M000073906

The Mysterious Case of the Missing Tuk-Tuk

A Bob Lowe Investigation

Zach J Brodsky

www.zachjbrodsky.com

ISBN 978-1-9164938-3-4

DEDICATION AND ACKNOWLEDGEMENTS

This is book is dedicated to Tobias and Jemima; thanks for encouraging me to take the time to focus on creating the first book in the Bob Lowe Series. This book was written in Thailand, India, and the UK. Bangkok continues to be a remarkable city and anyone who has visited will probably see a hint of realism even in the most absurd events in The Mysterious Case of the Missing Tuk-Tuk.

In common with Bob Lowe, I love this city and country that has been my home for many years. The first time I tasted *ba me moo daeng giaw naam* (Noodle soup with barbecue pork and dumplings) at the top of Sukhumvit 68, I knew I was somewhere special.

Many thanks to my editor Melanie Underwood for her hard work and for convincing me that I really should be hyphenating tuk-tuk!

Bangkok, November 2019

Glossary of Thai Words

555 – 5 in Thai is 'ha' so 555 in a text is laughing, ha haha
Aroi Maak – delicious
Farang – foreigner
Gaeng Maak – Very good
Ka, Khrap – Polite particles added to a sentence
Khaw Man Gai – Chicken with rice
Khun – A polite prefix to a name, Mr/Miss etc.
Maak – very when added to an adjective
Mai pen rai – Never mind, no worries
Mamasan – the woman who runs a bar with women for hire.
Moo Daeng – Barbecued Pork
Na – Particle used to soften a sentence
Narak – Cute
Nong – A prefix before the name of someone younger
Pee – A prefix before the name of someone older
Phuut Thai – Speak Thai
Soi – road
Ting tong – crazy
Wai – A greeting, placing both hands together
Yaba – Literally 'crazy drug' a cheap local amphetamine derivative
Ya ice – local name for crystal methamphetamine

ONE

Bob sat in his office and looked out at the people rushing through the mall. It was 10:30am, rather late for people to be on their way to work, he mused to himself. He called it his 'office', but on this day he was perched in 'Coffee Corner', a mediocre café in the corner of the ground floor of a small mall, near to Asok Skytrain station and attached to an office block. He had skirted by Starbucks on the way in and chuckled to himself. There were people paying a hundred baht and upwards for a coffee, some of the frappé-whatsits were nearer to two hundred. At Coffee Corner it was thirty-five baht for a hot black coffee. It suited Bob Lowe perfectly. He didn't always have an office base as such, but on this Monday morning he actually had some work to do, or potential work. Bob Lowe's Private Investigation service with its tagline of 'no job too small', had been running for nearly six months and business was slow off the ground, to say the least. Bob's low-cost, means-tested, limited advertising business model was

1

not proving totally effective.

"Time, my dear Susie. We must give it time," Bob had repeatedly said to his friend and supposed business partner, Susie Hoare. Her role as business partner was at present confined to listening to Lowe's musings and rants and allowing him to sleep on her sofa. He had quickly realised that with no guaranteed salary and his backup funds running seriously low, that rent was a luxury he simply couldn't afford.

Bob felt he had hit on a potential winning formula. He had heard in the past of *farang* (foreigners) in town who provided a service for overseas clients. They would check up on their girlfriends and confirm if they were still operating as 'bar girls', the term Bangkok gave to its bar-based prostitutes. This had proved quite profitable for some people. Who, Bob wondered, was providing the same such service to local women? Many an expat philanderer was to be found playing around, cheating on their girlfriends and Lowe felt he was just the man to assist.

He had explained this many times to Susie, trying hard not to reveal to her that he had an encyclopaedic knowledge of the bar girl scene in Bangkok. That was all in his past, he told himself.

"But, Bob, what can you charge them? Surely most won't be able to pay you enough for you to make a living."

"Aha. Well ahead of you there, Suze. I already have a payment plan worked out for my less financially secure clients. On taking the job I will charge one beer. One more beer for each day I am working the case and two beers on successful completion." Bob sat back, with a smug, satisfied grin on his face.

Susie was horrified. "Oh my God! You're actually serious!" Her trademark big toothy grin spread across her face, revealing her wrinkles in a sort of rippling effect.

Bob was deadly serious. When it came to beer, Bob Lowe didn't joke. He reckoned if he could get himself two or three of the low-income clients a week, and spend about a week on each case, then he could basically get free beer. This was of course supplementary to the paying clients he felt he would eventually be able to get.

Bob was already spreading the word in the bars he frequented, and with some of the girls he knew. What he really needed was for them to pass the word on to the ex-bar girls. He envisioned a sort of pyramid scheme where his potential client base would grow simply and exponentially. The ones who had settled with a boyfriend, these were the ones he needed to market his services to; this was where the money was at, in Bob's opinion. He was confident that he knew how these men would operate. They would never drink in the same bar or areas where they had met their partners for example. That was basic, and Bob knew all the alternatives and options.

He continued to wait in Coffee Corner. The previous night he had received a call from just such an ex-bar girl, Pim. Bob remembered her well. Pim had never forgotten him either; he was quite a unique character in all manner of ways, but there was one specific reason Pim remembered him. The night Bob had 'bar-fined' Pim, paid the fee to have her take leave from her bar job for the night, he had become encased with guilt. This was classic Lowe. Pim had told him that he was her fourth client of the day, and he'd suddenly felt a wave of sympathy. She explained that she was exhausted and that the previous client had not been a nice guy. She kept repeating that he was 'very strong man'. Bob wasn't sure if he wanted to enquire as to just what that meant. He just assumed it couldn't have been a good thing. Bob dropped her home in a taxi, gave her one thousand baht and went off in search of a massage; with happy ending of course. Such was the contradiction, the enigma that was Bob Lowe. Having felt guilty at hiring the services of a woman for sex, he took refuge in getting a massage with sex attached.

On the phone call, Pim had told Bob, "I remember you, you good man."

Bob had explained to Pim that they needed to meet so he could get all the details from her. Bob then rambled on, and most of it went over Pim's head, or at least beyond her level of interest.

"You see I don't have an office, Pim. My clients you see. Always consider the clients. Put the clients first. They don't want...*you* don't want to face the indignity of walking into a private detective agency. Mobile offices, or 'work spaces', it's all the rage these days, Pim, you trust me on this."

He had arranged to meet Pim at ten thirty in Coffee Corner. The fact that Pim could be up and about that early in the morning was a clear sign that she'd left the bar girl game. In the old days, Bob knew all too well, she'd have usually worked until three or four in the morning or if she'd landed a client she might be occupied until lunchtime the next day or, on occasions, even beyond that.

He almost didn't recognise Pim when she walked in. She looked like a normal person, he thought, and instantly scolded himself internally for such a crass thought. When Lowe had known Pim from her days working in Soi Cowboy she had tended to wear a tight crop top to show off her bust and a very short skirt with silver stilettoes. He realised how stupid he had been to expect that vision of Pim to walk into Coffee Corner at ten thirty to meet him.

She took a seat next to Bob. She had not been confident she would recognise him but at this time he was the only person in the small café.

"Ah, my dear Pim, you're looking a picture of health if I may be so bold."

"Hello, Khun Bob, how are you?" Pim replied, somewhat awkwardly.

"Couldn't be better, can't complain. This new business of mine really is very exciting. Boy do I have some big cases to deal with."

Bob had no idea why he started to begin this bullshit with Pim, she wasn't remotely interested and it certainly wasn't going to influence her in 'employing' his services.

Bob could sense her disinterest, not something Bob was always able to do, his lack of perceptive ability being one of his many faults. He thought it prudent to get straight down to business.

"So, what can I do for you, Miss Pim?" Bob got a cheap notepad out of his scruffy plastic bag, and opened to a fresh page onto which he wrote, *P014*. He chose the number fourteen at random, he didn't want Pim to think he didn't have multiple clients.

"You see, Pim, even my notes will be anonymous and entirely confidential."

"It about my boyfriend, I not know if he good man or bad man."

"I see, tell me more…" Bob wrote his first notes on this case: *Boyf, good or bad?*

"He home late many time. He say he working alway but I smell beer sometime. Sometime he go to holiday and he say it work. I not know. My friend say English teacher not need go away Saturday, Sunday."

"Yes, I see your predicament. Well you've come to the right man. This is an area of speciality for me." Bob tried to relax Pim. Put the client at ease. Rule number one on the Lowe PI list of rules.

Bob began to take down all the salient details. Pim had met this 'Brian' character in the usual bar she worked. It took Bob some time to ascertain that his name was in fact Brian, not an easy name for Pim to pronounce. At first Bob had heard 'By on' and had thought he may be named after Lord Byron, the great English poet.

"And thus the heart will break, yet brokenly live on," Bob quoted Byron, adding, "tragically apt, my dear."

Pim didn't know how to react. She did see Bob write the name down and corrected him. "No it not write this. It B-R-I-A-N, same like that."

Bob fought the temptation to try and teach Pim how to pronounce her boyfriend's first name.

"Now, what's his surname?" Bob tried to sound professional.

Pim explained that she wasn't sure what his surname was. A rather extraordinary state of affairs, but Bob wondered if this Brian could pronounce or spell Pim's full name.

Given that Pim and Brian had lived together for six months she gave remarkably little information.

She knew he taught English, but wasn't entirely sure where although she explained she could find out. She gave Bob a few first names of Brian's friends, but little else. In fact the only really concrete and useful thing was Brian's address, which was, nonetheless, a good place to start.

In Bob's means-tested system he had to enquire about Pim's finances. She explained that Brian gave her fifteen thousand baht a month out of which she had to pay bills (not including rent) and do the food shopping and general home expenses. The rest she could send to her family.

Bob explained that he'd need five hundred baht to retain his services, then he would charge five hundred baht for each week he was working the case, plus expenses. To Bob's relief, Pim agreed without complaint; he really didn't want to start having to negotiate his fee down.

Pim paid Bob a thousand baht upfront and Bob explained he would be in touch by the LINE messaging app, with necessary updates. Pim added 'LOWEPI' to her contacts' list and left Bob to get on with the case. Pim promised to text Bob if and when Brian was out in the evening. Bob had told Pim he would be following Brian on the way to work the next morning.

Bob sat back and slurped noisily on the dregs of his coffee. He politely indicated to the waitress that he'd like one more. "Bob Lowe PI. Who'd have thought it? Lowe is back," he muttered to himself at a volume that most people would be too embarrassed to talk aloud, in public, but Bob Lowe wasn't most people.

He chuckled at the extraordinary path his life

seemed to be taking, yet again. From being a first-class honours graduate in politics and economics, then a somewhat successful investment banker, he had proceeded to quit it all for a life of teaching English overseas. Initially Bob had embraced the job with great enthusiasm, almost passion. Within a year he was a grizzled, drunk, sex-pat or 'Nana Dweller'. Nana Dweller was a term exclusive to Bangkok, coined to describe the desperate men who spent all their time and money in the Nana area of town; one of Bangkok's notorious red-light districts. He had finally found a place where he felt he belonged – that is Bangkok rather than specifically the dodgy parts of town. The reality was that it was the dodgy parts of town where he invested most of his time. He spent years kidding himself that he was living the dream, before it all came crashing down. Those days were behind him now, although he had to keep reminding himself to prevent his mind wandering either misty eyed into the past or bringing him back down to a depression.

TWO

Suchart Lerksapong was a man of routine. He woke every day at 6:30am and brewed himself a strong cup of coffee in his kitchen, before heading out to sit in front of his small house. Suchart lived in a cosy wooden Thai house just off Soi Pipat, which was in turn just off Soi Convent in the fashionable Silom part of town. His small soi had managed to retain its strong 'Thainess' despite being a stone's throw from a part of town that was rapidly and inevitably gentrifying; giving in to the modern world of high-rise condos, transnational corporation head offices, and shopping malls. Suchart wasn't really one of those cantankerous old men who didn't like change, but he did miss the old Bangkok ways.

Suchart had lived in this same house for nearly forty years since he arrived as a young man from his home town of Lopburi where he was born and raised. His children had long since fled the family home, but still lived in Bangkok and visited often. His darling wife, Ploy, had passed away some three years earlier.

It was strange for Suchart at times, how quiet the house was. He still missed Ploy terribly, and thought about her all the time, but he had also become quite accustomed to living alone. He liked being able to do his own thing, watch whatever he wanted on TV, cook whatever he felt like eating and leave the house a mess at times. He used to laugh to himself when he noticed he hadn't cleaned up his coffee mug, thinking what Ploy would have said to him.

Suchart still earned a decent enough living from driving his tuk-tuk and he enjoyed the job. He'd chat a lot with customers, many of whom were regulars taking small trips around the area. For example, there was the young businessman who would often grab a quick ride to the Skytrain station (BTS), if there were no motorbikes available. Of course a good number of his customers were tourists, and Suchart enjoyed his attempts at speaking English with them. He felt proud of his ability to speak English, though in reality his grasp of the language was very limited.

He was also very proud of his job. Suchart Lerksapong was indeed a proud man. He felt that by driving a tuk-tuk he was desperately preserving an important part of Thai culture. His kids told him frequently 'people order taxis with their mobile phones these days', but Suchart was convinced the humble tuk-tuk still had a role to play.

On this particular morning, Suchart was awoken at 5am by an alarming noise outside. It was alarming that there was any noise at all. Nothing happened on this soi before 5:30am and even that was not a noise to wake you. He peered outside his upstairs window; Suchart's house was a simple two-floor design. He couldn't believe what he was seeing. He blinked to check he wasn't seeing things in a state of half-sleep. He clearly saw his tuk-tuk trundling down the soi. Stolen. He shimmied down the stairs, and only confirmed what he had seen from the window. The tuk-tuk which was always parked outside, tucked right into his house, had gone.

In his typically pragmatic way, Suchart decided he would go back to sleep and then contact the police first thing in the morning. There was little point trying to contact the Silom police at 5am, they'd still be dealing with the drunken happenings of a typical Bangkok night.

Crime on this soi? Suchart asked himself. It really was unheard of. In all his forty years the only criminal activities he could ever remember were local kids (sometimes his own!), pinching sweets from Nat and Ning's small 'Mom & Pop' store which was a few houses down. He'd never seen a policeman actually down his little sub-soi. Sure, on Soi Convent itself, but never down this quiet little alley.

Suchart felt a wave of melancholy sweep over him. What is happening to the world? He lay in bed and pondered that at least his beloved Ploy didn't have to face the devastation of a stolen tuk-tuk right outside their house.

Suchart re-woke at 7:10am, he'd had something of a lie-in, what with all the drama of the theft two hours earlier. He crept down his rickety old wooden staircase to make himself a cup of coffee, as he did every morning. This time he felt he needed to see once again the horrors of the stolen tuk-tuk. He peered out of the metallic netted grid-style front door and got another shock that he really wasn't expecting.

There, exactly as he had parked it the night before sat his tuk-tuk, in all its glory. After his delight and relief had passed he sat down with his coffee, bewildered. Had he dreamt it? Impossible! He remembered moving to the window, the wooden floorboards creaking and the unmistakable sound of his electric vehicle moving off down the soi. Those details could simply not be a dream, that was out of the question.

He sat. Thought. Confused, and almost amused. Was this some sort of prank? Who would play such a prank? In the past it might have been the sort of joke that Nat would play, but those days were long gone. Both Nat and Suchart were now the 'wrong side' of sixty and so it seemed an unlikely chain of events. No. Nat did not have the energy for these sorts of high jinks any more. Suchart sat and continued to contemplate what was going on. At that moment, Nat shuffled down the soi to join him for a morning coffee, as was usually the case.

"Morning, Daeng." Nat always called Suchart by his more common nickname, 'Daeng' the Thai word for the colour red. A nickname that had all but gone. If someone was called 'Daeng' you knew they were over sixty, and you'd expect them to be much older still.

They exchanged their usual morning pleasantries before Daeng went inside to brew another cup of coffee for Nat. He would bring the tin of condensed milk out for Nat, as he always did. Nat was quite particular about adding his own, as he wanted to get just the right amount of sweetness. They sat in silence, looking out at their street. Two men who had known each other for nearly forty years.

"My tuk-tuk was stolen this morning. No idea by

who. Or why." Daeng broke the silence.

Nat looked up, and just turned his head sardonically and stared right at the offending tuk-tuk.

Before he could speak, Daeng added, "Yes, I know. The thief returned it. Crafty blighter."

They continued sitting in silence, sipping their coffees before Nat chipped in, "Is he a thief then?"

"Or she," smirked Daeng.

"Who's she?"

"The thief."

"The thief was a woman?!" Nat was genuinely confused now.

Their conversation continued in this way for a few minutes before they both ended up laughing.

"Tuk-tuk's here. I wouldn't worry," was Nat's final word on the issue. Daeng nodded in agreement.

The two were such close friends that they were very comfortable with silent pauses in their conversation. They inevitably knew what the other was thinking and so sometimes those thoughts didn't need to be vocalised. It was amazing how much could be said with the odd raised eye, a glance or a smirk. It was almost as if they had a secret code and that the other could access a vast database of previous conversations. When a motorbike sped too fast down their little side street, it just needed a tiny, almost unnoticeable shake of the head and both Daeng and Nat would be revisiting many ranting conversations they'd had about motorbikes treating this tiny soi like it was the highway.

Their morning coffees and regular late afternoon meals were about as wild as life got for the two of them these days, but it hadn't always been that way. There was a time when Daeng, Ploy, Nat and Ning would sit out on their soi deep into the night; arguing, joking, and drinking lots of whisky. Life had been kind to them, they all recognised. They had always had enough money to live a good life and to raise their children in a manner that was better than their own childhoods. Daeng had begun working at the age of 14 in Lopburi, but in reality he had already been working for many years on the family farm before he began full time employment. His kids had no idea how good they had it, he often thought. Both his son, Boom, and daughter, Toon, had done well at school. Both had gone to university and thrived there. Daeng was so proud of their success. His best friend Nat would often remind him, "They get their brains and good looks from their mother!" Daeng always laughed, he was probably right.

Boom had just passed his thirty-fifth birthday. They celebrated with a family lunch at the Lumpini Park Hotel, a short distance from the family home. Boom was a deputy manager at another five-star hotel in town, but the Lumpini always held a magic, romanticised nostalgia in the family's hearts. Boom had been married for nearly ten years and had two wonderful children of his own. Daeng was so happy that in the last years of Ploy's life she had been able to spend so much quality time with her grandchildren. Both Boom and his wife, Noi, worked, so Noi would drop the children at Daeng and Ploy's early in the morning until they started going to school.

Boom's younger sister, Toon, was thirty-two and Daeng understood much less about her job. She was a marketing executive for a large Thai company but when she spoke with Daeng about work he had never been able to fully establish what it was she actually did. A hotel job he could easily imagine. He had seen Boom at work; he greeted customers, he answered their questions and dealt with complaints as well as organising the concierge and reception staff.

"A hotel is a hotel, simple!" he would often exclaim. Toon had always been very career focussed even before she had graduated from Chulalongkorn University. She was single, but happy with her life.

Daeng always said, "If my kids are happy, I'm happy and so I know somewhere Ploy is happy. That's all I need in life."

After thirty minutes of typically slow chat Daeng told Nat it was time he went to work.

"Another day scamming tourists, old man!" Nat chirped.

Daeng chuckled. "Never in forty years."

THREE

It was a beautifully cool January morning when Bob started to work on the Pim case. Bob loved this time of year. He didn't have to use his Lowe Sweat Time (LST) calculations to assess how long it would take for him to be drenched in unsightly sweat patches. In January he knew he could do a reasonable amount of walking outside, safely. April was a different story altogether. There was an intense heat to Bangkok at that time of year and Bob would often have to declare an LST of only a couple of minutes or if it became really serious, a matter of seconds, which would lead to a Lowe sweat crisis.

January though, he loved. It was often as cool as a British summer. He stood across the road from Pim's condo and tried to inconspicuously blend in. Eventually he saw Brian leave, pretty much at the time Pim had predicted. Bob made a careful entry of this into his small notebook before stuffing it into his pocket and beginning to follow Brian. He continued at a distance but also from the other side of the road, down to the Skytrain station. With an LST of 'N/A', Bob could happily keep up with the pace.

Bob was starting to make an initial assessment of Brian as he walked along the road. He had an air to him, Bob mused. An arrogance of sorts. He had seen this swagger many a time in the classic Bangkok expat – they thought they were something special. Bob wondered if Brian was one of those types who imagined he was immersed in Thai culture, as they boozed with other foreigners in British-style pubs in the popular expat areas of town. They tended to speak embarrassingly bad pidgin Thai, while believing that they were Thai speakers. Brian was unquestionably British. Bob could see it in his face, and of course Pim had already informed him of that anyway.

While in pursuit, Bob had to store all his notes mentally; he simply didn't have the time to keep stopping and writing in his notebook. Bob wondered if he should use his mobile phone as a recording device and take voice notes. He vowed to do a full feasibility study of that later on.

British, late thirties, Bob guessed. He also suspected Brian was one of those types who wanted to create an impression that he was a younger man. Although it wasn't easy to see from over the road he appeared to have a slightly angry, pinched look to his face. Possible West Ham fan, Bob considered as he began to imagine Brian as an arrogant cockney know-it-all.

They reached the BTS and Brian got on the escalator. On Bob's side there were stairs.

"Oh good Lord!" Bob exclaimed out loud and he began to race, insofar as Bob could race, up the stairs so as to keep tabs on Brian. His pace was just good enough as he did indeed reach the top shortly after Brian. Bob watched as Brian slipped through the entry gates with his Skytrain pass. At this moment Bob realised he would have to buy a ticket. "Remarkable," Bob muttered as he muddled through his pockets for some loose change. He had seen Brian go up the side for trains in the direction of Samrong, so Bob decided to select a ticket all the way to Samrong, the terminal station on this line. A few of the coins were rejected and he had to re-insert, much to his annoyance. Bob demonstrated his frustration with the sort of audible moans and grunts for which he was well known, among his friends.

Bob shinned it up the stairs and as he got to the platform a train was just pulling out of the station. There was no sign of Brian, so Bob's experienced detective skills ascertained that Brian had boarded the train. Sweat patches began to form on Bob's shirt (LST did not factor in running up the stairs at a BTS station). Bob got his notebook from his pocket and having already written down his general observations of Brian, he also added:

Target boarded Samrong bound BTS.
Target lost. Pursuit ended.

Nevertheless, Bob felt this was a start. He had learnt that Brian worked somewhere between Ratchatewi and Samrong. Not a bad first day on the case.

It had been nearly a year since his 'business' with his former friend, Alf Hayes, and while the knees didn't give Bob any trouble, his pride was still hurt. Looking back, Bob found it hard to believe he had agreed to go to Burma for a double knee replacement. Inside each knee was stuffed quantities of ya ice (crystal methamphetamine) that had made Bob a cool five thousand dollars. While the money had been useful, he later found out that Hayes had used him as a sap and had himself made a hundred thousand dollars from the deal. He hadn't seen Alf Hayes since the night Hayes had humiliated Lowe in a Nana bar, telling him just how much of a loser he was. Bob wondered if he should take it as a case. Was Alf Hayes in fact missing? Had he become too deeply immersed in the drug scene? It certainly was odd that he hadn't seen Alf in any Nana bars over the last few months, but he didn't want to think about his former friend anymore. Hayes' cruelty that night had triggered Bob to sink into a deep depression. Looking back now though, Bob realised that the infamous night with Alf Hayes was the beginning of the path to redemption that he saw himself on now. "No Hayes thoughts, Lowe." Bob had to remind himself that musing back over the Alf business was not at all healthy for him.

Bob had arranged to meet his old friend Susie Hoare for coffee and a spot of lunch at a café she knew down between Sala Daeng and Chong Nonsi station. He was feeling positive and upbeat as he descended the BTS steps and decided to enjoy the novelty of a tuk-tuk, rather than the ten to fifteen minutes it would take to walk. Tuk-tuks, while very much a symbol of Bangkok were rarely used by expats, particularly in these touristy parts of town. They were invariably a hassle, hot and dirty, and would inevitably involve a negotiation with a tuk-tuk driver, no doubt ready to screw the next unsuspecting farang out of his cash.

Khun Daeng was sat with his feet up and almost asleep when the tall and slightly scruffy Bob Lowe approached. Daeng was having something of a lazy day. He had nipped a couple of tourists down to the Neilson Hays library and done a few other short local runs. He didn't feel like he had much energy for a busy day of work. This apathy he had noticed ever increasing, the older he got. As a young man he would relish the chance to take a tourist around and act as a tour guide, but now he preferred the simple cash of short runs about the local area.

Bob spoke in Thai to Daeng, in an utterly bizarre Thai accent, but Daeng had heard this sort of Thai before and become quite adept at understanding. "Bai raan gafee soi pipat na khrap." (Go to a café on Soi Pipat). Daeng was old enough to still be impressed even when he heard bad Thai spoken by a foreigner, and he also knew these foreigners loved being complimented for their language skills. "Farang phuut Thai, gaeng maak." Daeng informed Bob he was impressed to hear a foreigner speak such good Thai.

Daeng proposed a fare of one hundred baht, about double what it should really be. He expected this farang to haggle him down.

"Marvellous, old boy," the affable Lowe agreed.

They managed a confused chat in part pidgin Thai and part pidgin English. Bob had specifically learnt how to say private investigator in Thai, as he felt this would impress people. So he managed to explain the basics of his new business venture to Daeng.

Indeed, Daeng appeared to be suitably impressed. They had already reached their destination but continued to talk. The bizarre content of the chat made it all the more confusing. Bob understood from Daeng that his tuk-tuk had been stolen.

"This tuk-tuk?" enquired Lowe.

"Khrap pom" Daeng cheerily confirmed.

"But we're in it?" Bob was genuinely baffled.

Eventually Lowe got the gist of the situation, that the tuk-tuk had been stolen, but then returned. A fascinating business, though he did wonder if he had misunderstood the details. Bob exchanged names and numbers with Daeng and had told him he could solve the case for a minimal fee.

"This is just the sort of case I eat up for breakfast, Daeng, my old pal." Bob was warming to the PR elements of his new job.

Susie was sat waiting for Bob and she greeted him with a big toothy grin. Often Susie's grins seemed false but Bob had noticed that since she had started taking antidepressants she had definitely seemed more relaxed and natural. He sat down and looked forward to a delicious lunch.

FOUR

Mint arrived for work at around one o'clock. She tended to vary her start times, but rarely would opt for a full afternoon session. Mid to late afternoon was usually a good start time for her. She could settle herself in, slowly working her way up to another evening punctuated by smiles and banter for Nana's drunks. In the past it was certainly not impossible for her to pick up a customer in the afternoon, for a quick 'short-time' session (namely a punter who just wanted a quickie, often less than thirty minutes). Even if that didn't materialise there was always the commission she would get from the bar if she was bought a drink by a customer. She found the afternoon punters were always straightforward, they simply wanted a quick bit of light relief. They were usually sober, which helped, and they were often reliable regulars. The only problem was an afternoon short-time customer was never a guarantee and so generally it would be much later in the evening she would get a paying client. After a few years of embracing her life as a bar girl, Mint preferred not to have too many customers in one week, finding that her body couldn't take it anymore and she didn't crave the money enough. If she was bar-fined two or three times a week that would be fine for her. Now she had gone further and reached a point where she was content with taking the cash from the commissions she earned for drinks bought in the bar, that was enough for her. Years of sex work had taken its toll and enough was enough.

As she walked into the bar she noticed the unusual regular, Mr Avi, in the corner. He certainly was unusual, she had known him from his regular visits to Bangkok over a number of years but she had never heard of him taking a girl home. He was a rarity indeed, he enjoyed the bar scene, he would drink for a few hours, have a meal, he would often tip well and tended to be on his way home by nine or ten o'clock. Mint liked him. She didn't tend to meet guys who seemed nice and pleasant, and who had no interest in purchasing her for the night. She immediately went over to say hello.

"Sawat dii, Khun Avi. How are you?" Mint bellowed cheerfully.
"Mint!" Avi was genuinely pleased to see her, he enjoyed a chat and Mint's English was pretty good compared to many of the waitresses.
"You know me Mint, can't complain."
"When you arrive Bangkok?" enquired Mint.
Avi told her he had been here for 2 weeks but had spent a few days down on the beach in Hua Hin, just to indulge in some much-needed pure relaxation. For

those days he had done nothing but read by the pool and eat some good food.

Avi Shielmann, was indeed an unusual character. An extraordinary and unique character perhaps. You only had to observe him for an hour or so in a bar to start to see his eccentricity reach the surface. Like most, when he had been drinking beer for a few hours Avi Shielmann would need regular visits to the toilet. Unlike most, Avi would never just walk to the toilets. He would dance, or specifically he would perform a light disco dance. Nothing too flamboyant these days, but noticeable, nonetheless. He would swing his hips, twirl the arms, perhaps do a mini half-spin. At sixty, Avi Shielmann still had it. If he wanted to, he still had the energy for a more serious boogie. If you were lucky enough to be in a Nana bar when Avi had been drinking for a couple of hours and a 1970s disco classic was played you were in for a treat. A full-energy disco jive was still well within the veteran's ability.

Avi Shielmann saw himself as a nomad. Israeli-born he had officially given up his Israeli citizenship as a political protest in his fifties and now travelled the world on a Swedish passport he had been able to obtain due to his time spent living in Stockholm. As a younger man he had a much more positive outlook and dreamed of a time when his nation would live in peace with their neighbours. He had long since given up even dreaming of that. Avi Shielmann's proudest moment in his life was his fifth place in the 1981 World Disco Championships. He believed then he would be part of a movement for peace in Israel.

Among his friends were Lebanese, Egyptians, Jordanians and those who lived in the occupied territories. "That's the power of disco," he would often say. "Avi Shielmann, dancing for peace," was another of his strap lines.

In the early 1980s he had teamed up with Mohammed Razzaq – the finest disco dancer to ever come out of Pakistan (in the opinion of Avi), and together he felt they would show the world that Muslims and Jews could live side by side. Avi and Mo couldn't though. They fell out, initially over purely artistic reasons – Shielmann felt Razzaq didn't understand the political possibilities of disco. Disillusioned by the split, Shielmann quit the disco scene in the mid-1980s and settled back into life as an accountant in Tel Aviv. He continued his quiet campaign for peace, and in the 1990s he began to have some genuine hope. But like Razzaq in the 1980s, Israel ultimately broke Avi's heart and he left for Europe.

FIVE

"You're looking radiant today, Susie."

"Oh, Bob, you old charmer!" Inside Susie was thrilled by this compliment, she need the boost; her self-esteem had taken quite a battering over the last few years, culminating in her walking in on her husband in a drug-fuelled sex session with a middle-aged Australian guy. It was the final episode in a marriage that had been petering out since soon after the wedding day.

Bob updated Susie on the complexities of the Pim case and the super news that she had paid some money upfront.

"This is the start, Susie, it's all coming together."

Bob had realised early on that the key to success in his PI job was going to be marketing and networking.

"You see, Susie, I need to take a more sophisticated, nuanced approach to this."

"How so?" Susie's interest was genuine even though she saw this whole enterprise as something of a counselling activity for her old friend.

"Well, Suze, I can't just rely on word of mouth. I can't just limit myself to BGM."

"BGM?" Suzie enquired.

Bob chortled. "Bar Girl Marketing. I should run courses on this stuff. I can see it now. Big posters around town. Bob Lowe – One day BGM seminars. Three thousand baht a head. Now where was I?"

This was a well-trodden path for Susie. Drinking and eating dinner with Bob and allowing him to get lost in his own thoughts. Their friendship had been developing for over a year since the unfortunate incident with Bob's one-time friend and Bangkok petty criminal, Alf Hayes. The event had left Bob emotionally crushed and feeling that he was without a friend in the world. Susie had been there for him and he had begun to realise she was actually a pleasant enough woman. He felt guilty for some of the more unkind ways he had treated her in the decade or so both had spent in the Big Mango.

He was careful with what he said to Susie when it came to his encyclopaedic knowledge of the bar girl scene, he didn't want her to know just how much of an expert he was. He was amazed by her naivety though. He had learnt during his first year in Bangkok that the idea of the impoverished girl selling her body as a last resort desperate way to earn cash was both a lazy stereotype and ludicrous over simplification. True, at his worst Bob had gone too far the other way. For years he effectively denied there was anything negative or exploitative about the bar scene in Nana. But people like Susie were blissfully unaware of the complexities of the Bangkok sex industry. Some of the women there were more akin to slick operators running small businesses. They balanced the day to day bar work with two or three long-term overseas boyfriends. Each man would pay a monthly allowance to his girl and typically visit for a few weeks each year. They often supported kids and family elsewhere in the country. They earnt good money and it certainly wasn't easy to balance three different relationships as well as not let on to their boyfriend that they were still working bars. Bob had also known of a young university student who simply wanted a pleasant enough partner to fund them through university. Who was being exploited there? Susie just had no idea. He had recently heard of an ex-flame, Pinky. Bob had become quite obsessed with her at one time, but she had never been interested in allowing him to hire her for a second night. Word was she had opened up a hotel in the north-east. He didn't ask for details but it was obvious there was a husband involved, or some other way that her bar customers were funding her new life. Bob once had an old mate who bought a bar business for a girl in Phuket. He was under no illusions about them being together, but he explained it to Lowe simply. "If you saw her, you'd have bought her a bar too." What he got in return was a couple of nice weeks with her each year down in Phuket. New Lowe was trying to have a more balanced view, and he had noticed some of the more misogynistic behaviour of the men, and was appalled. He had recently seen a heavily pregnant woman trying to pick up in the early hours from a street bar and being mocked by a couple of British guys. He was disgusted, but that was only one side of it. Like many things in Bangkok the reality was a lot more complex.

He continued to explain his BGM plans to Susie.

28

In short, while Bob drank his way down Soi Nana and its sub sois, he would leave his business cards on the wall or on tables in the bars. The cards were simple:

> BOB LOWE PI (Private Investigator)
> Bangkok's finest PI
> NO JOB TOO SMALL!!

"But you were saying you need to go beyond BGM, Bob."

"Correct, Suze! I've started leaving my card in tuk-tuks, hotels, apartment blocks. Wherever I can basically."

Business was still slow to pick up and Bob suspected, rightly so, that many of his cards were simply discarded.

"I don't ignore the old face-to-face marketing either, Suze; engage with the customers. The personal touch. Bob Lowe can go a long way on this personality. Watch!"

At this point Bob stood up and pulled a pile of business cards from his shirt pocket. Susie chuckled. The cards were all slightly different sizes and it was clear Bob had photocopied onto paper just about thick enough to be considered card, and then cut with scissors. Bob began to circle the small café.

"Bob Lowe PI. No job too small. Don't be shy, give me call." Bob liked his nice little rhyming ditty, but Bob didn't end there and the poetic delight was slightly diminished when he added, "Or email, Facebook, or even LINE text message. Well you got to these days. Thailand, eh? Contacts all on the back."

He'd usually get some sort of reaction. After all,

this was not the sort of thing one expected to encounter even in the wacky and bizarre nature of Bangkok.

"Could be some clients in this bunch." Bob sat down again, satisfied.

"In fact, Suze, I've just had a fascinating chat with a tuk-tuk driver called Daeng. He may have a case for me, but more importantly I've already hatched plans for him to spread the word about town. I've found my calling, Susie."

Susie looked intently at Bob. She wondered if he might actually be rather attractive, in a shabby sort of way. She was genuinely pleased to see him in such good spirits, but was a tad concerned that maybe he was flipping too far. Susie had battled with her own bipolar disorder for years, and had slowly become aware of the signs. Bob had quickly gone from a deep depression to a bustling positivity and a new project. Was he becoming delusional with this whole PI thing?

Much as Susie enjoyed her newfound friendship with Bob it did frustrate her that he so rarely enquired about *her* life and *her* problems. Their conversations always seemed to be very one way. Bob's new business, Bob's depression, and Susie's unstinting support to help him through it. He had even started to open up about his battles trying to wean himself off an addiction to Bangkok's bar girls.

She wondered if Bob even remembered how depressed she had been herself over the previous year. She was determined to try and turn the tables on him during this lunch.

"So, I texted Tong yesterday. I don't know why really." Susie opened the conversation. Tong was her ex-husband – well technically they were still married.

She hadn't seen him since that incident when she caught him with the Aussie guy. Her world had crumbled.

"Oh good Lord, Susie. What did he say?" Bob wasn't sure how one was meant to respond in these situations, but he knew it was important to try and demonstrate to Susie that he *did* care.

"Well, he ignored the message for hours. Which hurt even more. Finally he just replied to say he was fine and back up in Nong Khai. I felt so stupid."

"Matters of the heart, eh, Susie? They never do run smooth. Lord I'd know about that!" Bob tried to lighten the mood and laughed.

"We should have one of those pacts, and get married if we are still single in a few years!" Susie let out a ludicrously over the top laugh. It took Bob a moment to compose himself.

"Good one, Suze. Very droll. You see laughter really is the best medicine."

Susie could see in that split second a look of utter terror in Bob's eyes at the prospect. One night, years earlier, when both Bob and Susie were very drunk and, unknown to Susie, Bob had been unable to pick up the hooker he wanted, they spent a dreadful fumbling ten minutes in bed together. The humiliation complete when out of habit Bob left one thousand baht on the bed as he left.

"So TTM, tuk-tuk marketing and the like must go hand in hand with BGM."

And with that, Susie's feeble attempt to talk through her own issues and problems, was over.

Bob didn't notice the disappointment in Susie's eyes and took her at face value when she said, "Got to dash, Bob, I totally forgot I have a dentist appointment." She flashed another of her big, and this time slightly forced, toothy grins.

"Oh I see! Off you go, run along, Suze!"

The waiter came to clear Susie's coffee cup. Bob looked up at him and chuckled "Women, eh? Incorrigible beasts!" .

SIX

Avi Shielmann sat in one of his regular bars, nursing his second beer of the night. He tended to avoid the Thai beer brands as he found they had a tendency to give him a nagging headache or at least feel somewhat groggy in the morning. He stuck to Heineken, or San Miguel Light if he was concerned about calories. He was fascinated by Nana's bars and tended to drink there at least three nights a week as he pondered what he was doing with his life. On a wave of spontaneity he had quit his accountancy job in Stockholm for travel and retirement, or perhaps semi-retirement. Given that he hadn't worked since leaving the job, he was leaning towards thinking he was already properly retired. Financially, he'd done pretty well over the years, and had sold the small apartment in Tel Aviv that he'd inherited from his parents. He probably had enough to fund a simple enough retirement. But something was missing. He'd never married or had kids and one day he was sat in his Stockholm office looking out over the stunning vista of Stockholm's islands when he had a moment of clarity, an epiphany perhaps. He'd been staring at an email from a client concerning an unusual situation relating to business taxes. He was day dreaming, thinking about all the things he had done with his life; the glamour of the disco days, life in Tel Aviv, battles in Israel as a citizen strongly opposed to his own government, then moving to Sweden and taking up Swedish citizenship. What did he have to show for it? Memories, a comfortable life, and a lovely view from his office. Is that it? He wondered and then made an instant decision, something he had been grappling with for years. He replied to the email.

Dear Magnus,

Let me look into this matter this week. Then I will have to hand this to a colleague as I have decided to take retirement.
Yours,
Avi S.

Given that he was the only Avi working for Stockholm Finance Services, it amused many that he always signed off as Avi S.

He then got up, packed his small satchel-style briefcase with his empty flask (Avi always made his own coffee at home and brought it to work) and the plastic container that he'd brought his lunch in; a smoked salmon sandwich on rye with a smearing of horseradish. He told his secretary in broken Swedish that he was leaving early then went to speak to his boss Filip Nilsson. He'd expected Filip to try and persuade him to stay, but to his surprise Filip stood up, shook Avi's hand, and gave him a warm bear hug.

"You have my immense admiration, Avi."

Avi had never seen such warmth from the dour Swede.

Avi had visited Thailand many times over the years, regularly taking a two-week holiday during the Swedish winter. The decision to base himself in Thailand during his retirement was perhaps something of a cliché. Many Swedes visited and indeed also retired in Thailand and he had known many to come back waxing lyrical about the place and its people; this had triggered his first trip about five years earlier. On this day he felt fate was telling him to go back to Thailand, long-term. His client, Magnus, whose email he had been reading when he came to this momentous decision was married to a Thai woman and had three delightful children. Avi was always invited to their annual Christmas drinks and he'd always seen them as the perfect family. Then as he walked home he felt a craving for his favourite restaurant, a small café in Gamla Stan called 'Bangkok Kitchen'. As he approached, the owner Mr Wattana was putting up a new board with a special early evening offer.

"Mr Avi, new special offer, perfect for you I think." Wattana always spoke to Avi in English, they were both more comfortable in English than Swedish.

"Wattana, it might be just that." A light wind ruffled Avi's thinning hair and he grappled with it in a forlorn attempt to keep it looking neat and tidy.

He strolled in and sat at his usual table, where one of Wattana's many nieces came to take his order. He'd been a regular at Bangkok Kitchen for the last few years. It was his favourite eatery in Stockholm. There was a laid back, almost shabby charm to the place. Handwritten table numbers were taped to each table which were decorated with slightly old and faded plastic flowers. The food was fantastic, everyone who worked there was Thai, or at least Thai-Swedish, and most were part of Wattana's extended family. Avi could never remember who was the son or daughter of which of Wattana's relatives. It was genuinely authentic. Other so-called Thai restaurants were smarter and more expensive and when you investigated you'd often find the staff were Chinese or Malaysian; and the food was a bad stereotypical notion of Thai food.

He ordered his usual; crab cakes, green curry with steamed rice, and a pot of jasmine tea. Sometimes he'd finish off with mango and sticky rice and a couple of beers. He sat drinking his beer and looked at the stunning photos that adorned the walls, idyllic beaches, amazing temples, and the glory of His Majesty the King. He decided that yes, retirement in Thailand was surely the correct path. When he arrived in the kingdom some months later, it instantly felt like the right decision and Bangkok had become his base to explore the region.

"You thinking maak maak, Khun Avi?" Mint brought him out of his daydream.

"Life, Mint, life. How are you?"

"Always same, Avi. Happy happy!"

Mint always did seem happy. Avi often wondered if she really was. There was a real energy and buzz to these bars, and yes the girls did seem to enjoy themselves; often laughing and joking. Could they really be happy in such a career? Avi had long pondered this question on his visits to Bangkok.

At that moment his ears were alerted to a song

that began to play. *Just an Illusion* by Imagination. Avi had often described it as the last great disco tune. It was also the last song Avi had danced competitively to. He stood up, and the muscle memory kicked in. For the next four or so minutes he was transported back to Tokyo '83 when he danced for the last time in tandem with his disco buddy – Mohammed Razzaq. The sixty-year-old version of Avi was a bit rusty but he still had all the moves. People in the bar began to cheer and whoop, some were genuinely impressed, others just amazed at the sight of an old geezer dancing to himself in a moderately busy Nana bar. In the great scheme of things, a sixty-year-old Israeli with Swedish citizenship disco dancing in a Nana bar was just another run of the mill event for this part of town.

Avi sat back in his chair, utterly exhausted, sweat dripping down his face, yet exhilarated. He took a long swig from his beer that was just about still cold enough. A business card caught his eye. It was attached to the plastic container that housed his beer orders, with a flimsy piece of tape. Avi examined it carefully, *Bob Lowe PI.*

SEVEN

The Bangkok Women's Bridge and Lunch Society met weekly, on a rota of different locations. One week it was the Marriott hotel, another they had rented a function room at the Sukhumvit Prestige Hotel, or occasionally just in a pleasant café in one of the city's classier shopping malls. Wherever it was there was some planning required. There would usually be fifteen to twenty members coming on any one Wednesday. Officially there were over fifty signed up to the society, but some of those were actually working and so only came to monthly weekend functions.

Like any good society the BWBLS was heavily administered, with a treasurer, a club secretary, an events' organiser, a weekly bridge meet planner and a chairperson; their spiritual and actual leader so to speak. Marjorie Dubshott had been chair of the BWBLS since its inception back in the late 1990s when Marjorie arrived in Bangkok with her husband – Humphrey who was at the time, British Ambassador.

Officially there was an annual election of all those positions, but Marjorie had stood unopposed almost every year – there was one ugly business back in 2008 when a young trendy type, Sally Bamton, tried to join the society and modernise it. Marjorie saw off the challenge.

This Wednesday was a busy one, with twenty-three members attending and bridge starting at 10am in the lobby café of the Sukhumvit Prestige. Marjorie was a big supporter of this venue, as they always provided delicious biscuits with the coffee and the staff there were quick to replenish stocks. The lunch buffet was also very acceptable and excellent value, and they were happy to set up a mini buffet station in the lobby lounge exclusively for the BWBLS.

"Splendid as ever, Khun Suwit," Marjorie greeted the duty manager as she arrived, thirty minutes early as always. She felt it important to be there when the women arrived and also it was useful to check the tea and coffee station was all in order. She would then lay out the cards and notepads and pencils with her trusty driver Sapong.

"Oh, Suwit, you are an absolute gem, coconut delights! My very favourite." She slipped Suwit a five hundred baht tip.

"Thanks you, Khun Marjorie. Lovely to see you." Suwit spoke English to a very acceptable standard and so Marjorie always spoke with him in her native tongue. She did speak acceptable Thai but only used it if she had to.

"Suwit, Gladys is coming today. You remember Gladys? Oh she is marvellous, she's eighty-three you know. So we must look after her, she doesn't walk so well these days."

"No problem, Khun Marjorie. My staff will look after her, it very fine."

"Oh you are an angel, now where are the pencils, Sapong!" Marjorie stomped off to locate her driver, Sapong, who had neglected to lay out pencils on each table.

Next to arrive was usually Linda Foxsmith-Taylor. Marjorie had never liked the cut of her jib, and certainly found the double-barrelled surname a ludicrous attempt to social climb and sound upper class. In the eyes of Marjorie Dubshott you couldn't get more lower-middle class than Linda Taylor. Linda may have married into money having met Simon Foxsmith, but she couldn't disguise what she was. Nouveau riche. Marjorie could never stand such characters. Linda had tried so hard to lose her Birmingham accent, but it wasn't easy, which led to some wonderful passive aggressive exchanges.

"Lurvly… oh I do adore your Brummie accent Linda, it's so real. It must have been fascinating living in little Birmingham." Dubshott never missed the chance to get a dig at Linda, and she always referred to her as Linda Taylor or Linda Foxsmith.

Gladys Suprawongse certainly was a remarkable character and not just because she was an eighty-three-year-old who still had the energy and vigour to get herself around Bangkok. She almost never missed the weekly women's meet-ups. For Gladys it was more of a purely social event these days as her best bridge playing days were long gone. While she did still have a sharp brain she found her memory and concentration just weren't up to serious bridge playing anymore, but did still dabble occasionally. She was treated as a distinguished dignitary by the other women, and rightly so. Gladys had just celebrated fifty years living in Bangkok, and was well known in hi-so Thai circles. She had caused quite a stir in her native Kent in the late 1960s when approaching thirty she announced not only that she was marrying a younger man but that he was Thai and thus she was emigrating to Thailand. Her young suitor Chanathip Suprawongse was studying at LSE in London for a master's degree in applied economics before returning to Thailand to pursue a career in business and politics. His success was such that in the 1980s he had a spell as prime minister having been installed following one of Thailand's military coups.

His family were even less happy about him marrying a foreigner. His father's initial response was straightforward. "Absolutely out of the question. Enjoy this British woman and when you return home find a real wife, namely a Thai wife from the right sort of family."

The phone lines to Thailand weren't always clear from London but Chanathip had no problems understanding his father's message. It took him months to convince his parents that he was serious and eventually after a few years in Bangkok, Gladys Knight (yes that really was her maiden name!) had charmed not just Chanathip's family but the Bangkok social scene to the extent that she was a much sought after guest at hi-so functions. She had managed to slot neatly into upper class Thai life while also maintaining something of a down to earth way about her, which made her even more of a novelty. She even travelled on public transport, taking the Skytrain or underground MRT, which amused many of her friends.

"Oh, Gladys, you are an eccentric one!" Marjorie would often exclaim.

"Well, Marjorie, you've got to think about the environment these days. Absurd for me to be driven here when I can hop on the Skytrain for ten minutes."

Thai people were likewise amused when they saw the octogenarian wife of a former prime minister travelling by public transport, but many admired her for it. Chanathip was a much-loved figure in Thai politics, despite some rumours that he'd turned a blind eye to human rights abuses that took place. He was recovering well after a cancer diagnosis just after his seventieth birthday and strangers who recognised her often enquired about 'Khun Ball', her husband's rather bland nickname.

Gladys had been known for her cooking. Her specialities were her desserts and she had adapted many of her recipes to add a Thai flavour. Her famous chocolate cake had a gooey coconut filling and was usually topped with sliced mango; her British take on the Thai classic of mango and sticky rice. Her cookbook 'Khunying Gladys' Thai-British Classics' still sold well some twenty years after publication. Gladys was one of the most popular women in the BWBLS and was almost universally loved by most people she met. Marjorie Dubshott despised her for it. She played along with the 'isn't Gladys marvellous' line, but inside she seethed; bitter and just a little jealous. She longed to find just one person who would also see the irritating side to Gladys's near perfectness, but alas, to date she had not. She was the only member of the BWBLS to have ever had the title 'Khunying' a grand title bestowed on the great and the good by the monarch each year. For Gladys to have earned that title, as a foreigner, was even more remarkable. It was rather like being a Lady or a Dame in Britain, but somehow in Thailand this was much more of an honour. Marjorie felt Gladys had a false modesty, at times proclaiming that she really wasn't concerned with titles. At other times Marjorie had heard Gladys reminding people that she was in fact *Khunying* Gladys Suprawongse, before then adding, "Oh, I am only joking, of course you can call me whatever you'd prefer."

EIGHT

Bob was sitting on Susie's sofa, binge watching a TV series that he had already seen in its entirety, when he next got a message from Pim. The previous day he had successfully followed Brian to the language school where he worked, only to realise that he could have simply asked Pim to find it out for him and give him the address. However, he was pleased to have succeeded and he felt it was all good experience for this new career of his. Pim's text to Bob was just to inform him that Brian had said he would be late home from work as he planned to have dinner with colleagues at the end of his teaching day. It was three in the afternoon when Pim texted, which Bob felt gave him plenty of time to be ready outside Brian's workplace to follow him. Bob knew the language school game well and felt it was likely Brian would be working until after five. A core teaching time was the after school hours as many kids would be sent by their ever-ambitious parents for intense English lessons after a full day at school. Bob had worked for many years in such places where he'd teach all weekend and then on two or three weekdays he'd tend to work only from three pm until around six, or occasionally as late as eight. It suited Bob perfectly, he had the mornings to work off a hangover. On Saturday and Sunday he invariably had to start work at eight in the morning, which was sometimes hard going, though it was true that one of his genuine skills was his ability to function after a major drinking session. Nonetheless, if Bob had an evening off from the heavy drinking he'd always try to ensure it was a Friday or Saturday. Again, he liked this system as the bars would be a bit too busy for his liking on those weekend nights anyway. 'It cramps the Lowe's style' as he'd told many an acquaintance over the years.

Bob Lowe was something of a bizarre contradiction, as were so many of Bangkok's characters. On the surface he could be dismissed as a 'Nana Dweller'; one who spent most of their time drinking in Nana's seedy bars and enjoying regular paid-for sexual encounters.

Although the new Bob; Bob Lowe PI, was desperately trying to become a reformed character, it was still true that the Nana Dweller tag would have been accurate for most of Bob's decade plus years in Bangkok. Bob seemed a simple stereotype to some; certainly he lacked social skills and logic, but scratch beneath the surface and you'd find someone with a considerably higher than average IQ who once had a promising future as an investment banker in the City of London. He quit it all for English teaching in Bangkok and he had presumed the years of heavy drinking and heavy antibiotic consumption (to tackle the inevitable STIs he regularly contracted), had deadened his intellect significantly, though he could still at times show flashes of the brains of the young man who graduated from one of the UK's leading universities with a first-class honours degree. That would not be apparent to anyone who'd see him sprawled on Susie Hoare's sofa in frayed boxer shorts, sweating profusely and struggling to change channels via the myriad remotes Susie had.

"Unfathomable," he'd mutter to himself as he inadvertently turned off the digibox, in turn cutting off his series.

Bob took this as a sign that it was time to head to 'work' and follow Brian on his night out. He was fortunate that there was a small café which was a good vantage point for viewing the entrance to Brian's workplace, so he could patiently watch the door and casually attempt to merge into the background. The language school didn't look as most people would imagine a school, it was in fact situated in a ten-storey office block with the 'XYZ Language School' taking up most of the sixth floor. Brian emerged with two others shortly after six o'clock and Bob praised himself out loud for his accurate prediction. "Spot on again, Lowe!"

Bob followed the trio to the Skytrain and with a new found slickness he was able to smoothly follow them onto the train. Bob had purchased a pass known as a 'Rabbit Card' and charged it up with five hundred baht for a number of trips. Since Brian and his friends didn't know Bob, he felt confident he could board the same carriage as them, and with standing room only he found himself within earshot so he could listen in to their conversation.

Of Brian's two friends one was a little younger,

possibly late twenties or early thirties and Bob used his skills to establish the younger man's name was Paul. The other chap was heavily overweight and looked uncomfortable in a tight-fitting shirt and tie combo. His neck was trapped by the collar with some of his skin just squeezing out over the top. Bob hadn't managed to ascertain his name so he scrawled *fatty* in his notebook. Brian seemed to be enquiring with Paul about his latest romantic conquest.

"Yeh, I may see her again. She could be possible relationship material, maybe," Paul said confidently.

"Nice one, mate. I've told you before, get a regular one at home," Brian responded.

"I mean, she clearly likes me. It's not about money when she's with someone like me. Of course, like most, she'll do fat farang just for the money, oh er, sorry, mate," Paul turned to fatty, "but with me it's obvious that she is really into me."

Fatty sighed, he'd clearly heard it all before. The conversation continued like this for a while and Bob chuckled to himself at what he considered Paul's startling naivety. Bob scrawled in his notes against Paul's name *possibly first year in Bangkok*; against fatty's notes he'd written *miserable, old hand, probably married.*

They disembarked at Nana, which was no surprise to Bob. He really felt he was getting good at this PI lark. What did surprise him was that they headed in the opposite direction he'd expected and wandered down Soi 11, rather than Soi 4 – the beating heart of Nana's bars and commercial sex industry.

The three strolled into an Indian restaurant. Bob examined the menu outside for a good five minutes while he could check that the trio were settled in and ordering a meal. Bob knew he'd have at least forty-five minutes before there was any chance of them emerging. He wandered the soi, popping in and out of every 7-Eleven. In one he'd buy himself some chewing gum. In another he made a ludicrous show of pretending they didn't have what he wanted. What he did want was to take full advantage of the air conditioning, even though it was a relatively cool evening by the intense standards of Bangkok. He timed his return to the restaurant fairly well but still had to surreptitiously wait for ten minutes before the three friends exited.

Fatty hailed a taxi and Brian joked, "Back to the trouble, eh?!" Bob gave himself two metaphoric pats on the back and furiously ticked in his notebook. One for correctly predicting that fatty was a downtrodden married man but also Brian's use of the cockney rhyming slang trouble (trouble and strife – wife) increased the likelihood that he was indeed a West Ham fan!

Bob followed Brian and Paul as they walked down Soi Nana and went into the absurdly named 'Bar Bar Bar'. Bob followed and sat at the table next to them. He hadn't been to 'Bar 3', as it was affectionately known by regulars, for a while and so he was enjoying the change of scenery. The music was a little noisy and Bob found it difficult to eavesdrop on Brian's conversation so was subtly trying to shuffle his chair ever closer. After only about half an hour, and to Bob's utter horror, Brian looked at him and spoke. "Alright, mate. I saw you on the BTS earlier, small world."

"Eh? Who me? Really! On the BTS? Was I? I mean, I was, yes, yes. Good Lord. Remarkable. Oh yes, the BTS, wonderful system, always use it. Hardly a surprise you saw me." Bob was stumbling his way through this, and luckily Brian interrupted him and invited him to join his table. Once he had calmed down, Bob realised this might actually be a great opportunity to learn more about Brian. He felt like one of those FBI agents going undercover in the mafia. Inside Bob was feeling incredibly excited.

They chatted in a relaxed way. A lot of small talk, assessing the quality of the girls in the bar. The next sticky situation for Bob was when one of the waitresses, Joy, came over to speak to him.

"Hello, Khun Bob, not see you long time, na."

"Oh, Joy! Yes, you know me, I don't drink often."

Joy laughed at what she assumed was a joke.

"How your private police job?" Joy enquired.

"Anyway, lovely to see you, sweetie, run along Joy, three more beers for me and my new mates."

The cat was out of the bag though, and Bob was going to have to use all of his limited supply of cunning.

Brian and Paul immediately asked about his police work.

"Oh yes, well I do a bit of PI work." He then added in hushed tones, "You know I check out some of these girls for their boyfriends, make sure they're not still working the bars." Bob felt this was a suitable smokescreen. Though later he pondered why he didn't say something boring like he was involved in analysing financial data for fraud cases.

"Really?! I've heard about this sort of thing. We better both take your number!" Brian smirked and nudged his mate Paul. Bob was getting in deep and after a few hours drinking, Paul and Brian both left with one of Bob's DIY business cards.

NINE

It was just approaching dusk as Daeng sat down in his kitchen ready to enjoy one of his favourite meals; Khaw Man Gai – chicken with rice. Despite the simplicity of the dish it was as much a favourite for Daeng as it was with so many Thai people. He had been eating from the same stall on his soi for over twenty years. There was something really special about it and in particular the rich flavour of the clear soup that accompanied the main dish. Khun Tan who ran the stall was the master of the Khaw Man Gai as far as Daeng was concerned. He was treating himself to a mixture of half fried chicken and half steamed chicken, all perfectly sliced. He painstakingly prepared the meal back in his kitchen, as in opening all the containers. Chicken and rice on his plate. Two small bowls into which he poured the small bags of sauce (one sweet and one spicy) and finally a bigger bowl where he emptied the plastic bag tightly fastened and full of steaming soup. Daeng was aware of the modern complaints about the amounts of plastic being used, but he didn't see how there was an alternative when Thai food required so many different accompaniments. He figured Thailand needed to be a special exemption when it came to a global campaign to decrease the use of these plastic bags and takeaway packages. Finally he added his special touch; he cut the accompanying cucumber into small chunks and dropped them into the warm chicken broth. He looked lovingly at this perfect ensemble and for a brief moment he understood why his two children both insisted on taking photographs of their food almost every time they ate! He almost took out his mobile phone and he chuckled to himself at the very idea. He also chuckled a bit more as he thought of the endlessly repeating conversations he'd had with Boom and Toon when they insisted on pointing their devices at their meals. Although he had noticed on the rare occasions that *he* cooked for them their phones remained firmly in their pockets. Then he'd change his tack.

"Oh, *this* meal you *don't* want a photograph of to send to your friends!"

His kids would raise their eyebrows in unison. He smiled at this thought which quickly became a sigh and a grimace as there was a tap on his door just as he was about to taste the first bite of the delicious and glistening chicken and rice. He was even more irritated to see his son Boom at the door. Boom waied his father as a sign of respect, by placing his hands together as in prayer and lining his thumbs just below the nose, the higher up the face the more respect shown. "Hello, Dad," he cheerily added.

"Why did you knock? I'm just sitting down to some of Tan's Khaw Man Gai," he admonished his first born.

"I was brought up better than to just burst into people's homes!" Boom replied with a glint in his eye.

"Not by me, you weren't!" The verbal rallying continued.

"Gin khaw ru yang?" Daeng enquired if Boom had eaten yet. As the words were exiting his mouth, Daeng knew this would end with him giving up his meal. He imagined the words of his beloved Ploy. "Let Boom eat, you can get Khaw Man Gai from Tan any day!"

Boom made a pretence of not wanting to take his dad's dinner, but he knew the old man would insist. Luckily Daeng knew he could call Khun Tan and she would get one of her helpers to deliver a fresh portion.

"Hi, Tan, it's Daeng here. Same again, please. Can someone deliver?"

"Oh! So hungry today!"

"Boom's here." No other words were needed and Tan giggled. Within ten minutes a young chap knocked on the door with a fresh helping and Daeng went through the same rigmarole of emptying it all out into bowls as his son tucked into his meal.

"I forgot how amazing Tan's Khaw Man Gai is, still the best." Boom talked as he ate.

"It is so, but I don't need to see it in your mouth too," Daeng spoke sardonically, with a hint of a frown.

"I could probably eat a second helping." Boom looked at his dad and laughed. "I'm joking!"

The two chatted for some time. Daeng enjoyed hearing the latest from the hotel. He was so proud of what his son was achieving with his life. There was always some drama with the reception staff or the hotel maids and he wondered how stressful it must be having to manage all those staff. In *his* work he only had to worry about his tuk-tuk breaking down. Though he had also helped Ploy as she cooked noodles on a small stall outside the front of their house. Ploy had continued to make noodles until she become too weak from the sickness to continue. Her Ba Mee Moo Daeng (egg noodles with barbecue pork) was as legendary as Tan's chicken rice.

"What's the latest in the tuk-tuk game?" Boom asked.

"Tuk-tuk was stolen," Daeng said, matter-of-factly.

"It's right outside, Dad."

They then had the same conversation Daeng had had with many over the last two days. Though whereas others believed Daeng and became curious about what was going on, he noticed that his son immediately thought his dad had dementia setting in.

"Are you sure you're okay, Dad?"

"No… but I'm the same as I've ever been! Don't you start telling your sister otherwise."

"Maybe think about taking some time off? Take a rest," Boom slightly condescendingly suggested.

Daeng explained for the umpteenth time that he enjoyed working and he was far too fit and healthy to consider resting or going part time.

"You kids today, you don't know what hard work is! My job is a piece of cake compared to my parents!"

Boom put fifteen thousand baht on the table, the usual monthly amount he gave to his dad and Daeng gave him a warm hug.

"You really don't have to worry about me you know, but it's good that you do," Daeng said sentimentally.

It was a sign of Boom's success that he was able to

give his dad such an amount each month. He remembered the days when his salary was too low and he struggled to give five thousand. He looked at the tuk-tuk as he walked out, and wondered if it really was possible that his dad had imagined it? What was the other explanation? No one would bother to steal a tuk-tuk to race around Silom for an hour!

Daeng put the dishes in the sink and decided he would wash up in the morning. A luxury he could afford himself now that he was a widow. Ploy wasn't a nag as such, she just knew that Daeng hated having to wash up in the mornings, so she'd always suggest he did things before going to bed.

He put on the TV and watched the news and some absurd soap opera that he found absolutely unfathomable, but it reminded him of Ploy so he liked to have it on, even if it was just background noise. The plot was predictable but nonetheless he could never completely follow it. After a while he settled himself in bed upstairs, read for a bit and then quickly fell asleep.

For the second time in a matter of a few days he was awoken early to the sound of his tuk-tuk scuttling down the soi. This time he pinched and lightly slapped himself to be sure that he was awake and not imagining things. He was actually quite amused this time, yet very puzzled. He fumbled for his phone and tried to remember the name of the British guy who was working as a private investigator. His brain wasn't forthcoming, but he searched through his old wallet and stuffed inside was the scruffy business card that Bob had given him. He sent Bob a simple text, *I Daeng tuk-tuk thief again.*

TEN

Bob was very excited to receive the text from Daeng, for the first time in his fledgling new career he had two cases going, concurrently! He'd soon be over-worked! He arranged to meet Daeng at his house later that day. That in itself was no mean feat involving texts in phonetic Thai and struggled phone calls. Bob eventually was confident that they had arranged to meet at five pm. He called his friend Pat and asked if she would be kind enough to help him with translations, promising he would take her for some food after the meeting. Bob was quite proud of his friendship with Pat, one of the few genuine local friends he had after a decade or so in Thailand. Pat had worked in the admin office of the first language school Bob worked at in Bangkok. They'd instantly got on well, Pat finding Bob's many odd and quirky ways very amusing. For many years Bob dreamt of being in a relationship with her but he had never had the confidence to actually ask her out. They had slipped into being work friends and Bob had accepted that, but still occasionally he had regrets and 'what if?' thoughts. He sat down on a bench in Benjasiri Park and pondered his next move. Just at that moment his life became that bit more complicated as his phoned buzzed – another new LINE message.

Hi, Bob. It's Brian here. You gave me your number the other night. Can we meet? I may need your services.

Bob was initially panicked. This was surely a recipe for disaster, if not unethical. Though he had no idea if there even *was* an ethical code among private investigators. He pondered this for a moment before deciding that his whole business was somewhat unethical. He started to consider that there may be a positive side to all this. His case with Pim would be solved simply – he would insist to Brian that he needed to know all the background details of his life with complete honesty. Somehow he needed to ensure he found out about Brian and his relationship with Pim, even if Brian's case proved to be completely unrelated to his girlfriend.

Within the space of just a few hours Bob suddenly had three clients. He gazed around the small park, a regular place to sit and think. At eight o'clock in the morning there were still a few people jogging and exercising but it had very much thinned out. A small lake in the centre was the focal point of the park and there was always a pleasant calm here despite being nestled between the Emporium shopping mall, a major hotel and the busy Sukhumvit Road. Bob always had a Zen-like calm when in this park, well almost always. He had got into a frightful business one Loy Krathong day. The festival of Loy Krathong saw Thai people float (loy in Thai) a small boat made of leaves (Krathong) to wash away their troubles. It was traditional for people to fill the boat with hair, fingernail clippings, and among other items a few coins. At the far end of the lake the local neighbourhood kids would collect the krathongs and empty them of their coins. He wanted in on the act so stormed around to the kids and shouted 'bai leaw' to try and get them to go away. They laughed. Bob nudged his way to the edge of the lake and tried to grab a krathong. Inevitably he slipped and, being unable to swim, he flapped about screaming in panic before a nine-year-old boy dived in to rescue him. He trudged home, soaking wet, to many giggles and odd stares from the locals.

The Emporium Mall was another of Bob's favourites and specifically the fifth floor where he would go on one of 'Bob's Gourmet Food Walks'. On a visit there he'd take advantage of as many free samples as he could. Typically he would taste some cheese, salami, sometimes a bit of cake or bread. He'd never buy anything, muttering comments like, "Oh dear, a tad too salty for me, what a shame." One of the chapters of the never finished book 'Bob Lowe's Thrifty Bangkok Living' was entitled 'There *IS* such a thing as a free lunch; how Bob's gourmet food walks will have you eating for nothing.'

After a few hours milling about the park and Emporium he hopped on the Skytrain and soon found himself sitting opposite Brian in the very café he'd sat stalking him a week earlier.

"So, Brian, how can I be of service?" Bob tried to sound professional.

"Well, I'm sure you can guess, mate. It's my girlfriend, not sure if I can trust her."

"I see. I see. Now is she also British?" Bob was

desperately trying to imagine what he'd ask if he didn't already know who his girlfriend was.

"Nah, mate. Pim's Thai."

"Okay. Got it. Why not indeed. That's P-I-M, I assume?"

Bob was laying this on a bit thick. Brian just nodded.

"So, M for Mother? I've known a few Pin's in my time, I can tell you!"

Brian explained that he'd been living with Pim for six months, and that recently she'd been acting rather strangely. He was certain that she was texting a guy.

"Why do you think that? If I know girls like Pim, she'll be constantly chatting with her girlfriends."

"What do you mean, 'girls like Pim'?" Brian said slightly defensively.

"Thai girls, mate! They love their phones." *Phew, close one,* Bob thought to himself. "So can I ask where you and Pim met?" An innocent question he thought. Well it was certainly an innocent question in normal society, but in Bob's time in Thailand he had soon realised it was an unspoken rule that you didn't ask such a thing. He had met many a guy who had gone to great lengths to tell you effectively that their girlfriend wasn't a prostitute. A bizarre state of affairs. He remembered once being introduced to a friend of a friend. The friend introduced his girlfriend as, "This is my better half, we met at the make-up counter in Central Chit Lom, of all places. Would you believe that, eh?" A very odd way to begin a conversation.

Brian also realised the charged nature of this discussion.

"Oh no, mate, nothing like that. She worked in the office near my school, I met her there. She's not one of those girls, mate."

"No, of course not, I see." Bob maintained a serious face but chuckled inside. Another of those guys who didn't want to admit that he'd met his girlfriend down in one of Nana's bars.

"So, this is a slightly delicate matter, you understand I must ask…"

"Go on…" the cockney waited in anticipation of this tricky question.

"Well, Brian, I hope you understand it's important I know everything, so I have to ask… are you faithful to Pim?"

This was it. Bob's chance to solve his first case with just one question.

Brian angrily retorted. "I'm not one of those guys, mate, of course I'm faithful to Pim."

"That's good to know. In my wide experience of these sorts of cases, if one person cheats then the other often is too." Bob was getting into a confident stride.

Brian again insisted he was faithful and explained he just felt Pim was lying to him and being secretive about who she was texting. Bob explained his fee structure (the expat one) and Brian paid an initial five thousand baht retainer. Before Brian left for work Bob added, "Remember, mate, you can tell me anything, it's all confidential. The Lowe Oath. Clients first. Always."

For his own amusement Bob gave Brian the code of *P014a*, as if this was a sub-case of the case Pim had hired him for. In effect it was. He laughed out loud. He was really doing this. Even Bob had believed that Bob Lowe PI was an unrealistic and ludicrous pipe dream, but now he may have to rethink that. He had five thousand baht in his pocket to help him ponder.

He texted Susie. *I'll nip to the supermarket after my 5pm appointment. Anything we need? I've just been paid.*

Susie's reply was simple, a sticker of a shocked dog caricature, sweating. She was as shocked as Bob at this development.

Bob smiled again. He'd not felt this happy for years. "Good day to you," he said to the waitress, doffing his cap as he left.

Bob was pleased to have an excuse to meet up with Pat. He didn't find it easy to manage a friendship with a woman, least of all one with whom he had once harboured romantic ambitions. With men it was easy, he'd just suggest meeting up for a beer or to watch the football. He just didn't feel as comfortable with female friends. What if she thinks it's a date? would go through his mind. But then maybe that was a good thing. He'd then go through a whole series of ifs and buts. Of course he knew that in the twenty-first century it was perfectly normal for men and women to be friends, but sometimes he was more like a seventy-year-old man than someone in his forties, in terms of his outlook on life. He'd all but given up hopes of marriage or children and although he'd never admitted it to another soul, it had been fifteen years or so since he'd had a sexual encounter that wasn't paid for. He'd often wondered how different his life might have been if he'd had the guts to ask Pat out when he first started working with her. At that time he hadn't really considered if he'd like a girlfriend and then he had quickly got himself fully immersed in the bar girl scene of Nana and Soi Cowboy. He had seen nothing like it before. Bob had long accepted that beautiful women were way way out of his league. That had all changed when he arrived in Bangkok, suddenly he was surrounded by these drop-dead gorgeous women and they all seemed to want him! Whatever *it* was, Bob seemed to have it. As the years moved on, Bob quickly began to drop the delusions and became something of a hardened cynic. He'd gone through stages where he had convinced himself that it wasn't just about money for some of the stunning women he had picked up. "It's a lot more complicated," he'd begin to lecture newbies in Bangkok. Then he'd explain that since many of the women came from the poorer regions of Thailand that he was in effect doing his bit for poverty. For a time he believed this. He went through phases of guilt when he realised just how difficult life was for some of the girls he picked up. But he had become addicted and it wasn't easy to let go as he attempted this path of redemption and rehabilitation. The PI work would help, if it continued to keep him busy.

He met Pat by Sala Daeng BTS station and the entrance to the Central shopping mall. He wasn't sure if he should greet her with a hug and kiss 'European style' and in the end he awkwardly shook her hand. "Wonderful to see you, Nong Pat."

"Hello, Pee Bob... detective Bob!" Pat joked.

"Good Lord! Well, I'm not sure about that just yet, Pat!"

Bob took on a serious and almost professional tone as he briefed her about his new client.

"Khun Daeng, wonderful chap! Real old school. English a bit dicey, my dear, and well, you know my Thai; phuut passa Thai mai geng!" A stock phrase that many foreigners used to express that they didn't speak

Thai very well. They were secretly hoping of course that merely uttering these words would have the effect of impressing people in their grasp of the language.

Pat chuckled. She did enjoy Bob's quirky awkward ways, uncomfortable in his own skin at times.

They battled their way down Silom Road and into Soi Convent. It was rush hour; people were heading for the Skytrain to go home or heading for some post work drinks and food. There was an art to navigating Bangkok streets in rush hour and many farang hadn't learnt it even after years in the city. Bob was, of course, one of those. He thought he had mastered the art at times, but he was still forever bumping into people. The key was the golden rule, 'Do not try and walk too fast!' If you did you would be forever bumping into what Bob called SMTs 'Slow Moving Thais'. Bob was also frequently wound up by youngsters walking around while texting or 'surfing the instawhatsits' or his absolute bête noir, those who stopped at the top of escalators or by a shop door to chat. "Has the whole world gone mad?! Can no one follow the simple rules of life?" he had been known to exclaim out loud on a busy Bangkok street. Bob had learnt *some* of the skills over the years and he sort of loped about town with his own version of a 'mai pen rai' never mind, attitude. As they walked by an Irish pub, Bob pointed to a noodle stall.

"That, my dear Pat, is one of the top five Ba Me stalls in this fair city. Lowe endorsed."

"It's okay, but better ones near my home," Pat matter-of-factly replied.

"Friendship over!" One of Bob's favourite jokes. He insisted they would eat there after the client meeting.

"It's the pork, Pat, lovely rich flavour."

"Just normal," answered Pat.

This time Bob was genuinely irritated by Pat's dismissive indifferent attitude to the pork noodles. The foot traffic thinned as they walked into Soi Pipat and eventually they found the small sub soi that Daeng lived on.

As soon as they sat down at Daeng's table, Pat completely took over, chatting at great speed with Khun Daeng. She had completely ignored Bob's 'let me take the lead' advice and was just off in her own style trying to obtain all the necessary details. Bob made a mental note to castigate Pat for her lack of professionalism.

Bob was utterly lost but did his best to maintain the pretence that he was following by just nodding and barking out any word he understood.

"Thief, yes… today… tuk-tuk… car? What? Aha, morning… yes, yes… thief! What's good? Who?"

After thirty minutes they left to get some of the noodles. Bob confidentially declared that he had, "…pretty much got all of that, but perhaps just to be clear you could debrief me?"

Pat had noticed Bob was earlier genuinely irritated at her apathy and apparent dismissal of his comments about the Ba Me noodles at this stall so after a few bites she declared, "You know what Bob, you are right, this is very good!"

Bob beamed. "Aha! Trust The Lowe! Aroi maak!"

Pat fully updated Bob. Actually it was straightforward, if rather bizarre. It seemed that virtually every morning Daeng's tuk-tuk was taken at around five am and returned before six thirty. In an added twist the thief had started occasionally leaving a hundred baht note, wedged in the steering wheel. Pat found it very puzzling.

"Ah yes. Nothing new for The Lowe. Joyriders no doubt. This should be easy. Or should I say, elementary, my dear Pat." The joke was lost on Pat. Bob continued, "A case likes this requires careful observation and watching. What we in the business call a *stakeout*. I'll be there at five am tomorrow and I will have this sorted in no time."

Pat was impressed. It did seem Bob knew what he was doing and had indeed shaped himself an exciting new career. At that moment his phone buzzed. Bob checked the message.

"Hi, I saw your card in Nana. I have a unique case for you. Can we meet? Avi Shielmann."

Bob was incredibly excited and Pat could tell he was trying to look calm when he said, "Another new client. It's just non-stop for Lowe PI. Tom Selleck step aside."

Bob said his goodbyes to Pat and they agreed not to leave it so long to meet up again. Bob told her that, with his business rapidly growing, he may well have more work for her.

At five the next morning Bob was stood tucked into the house opposite Daeng with a clear view of his tuk-tuk. "This will be easy," he'd explained to Susie on getting home the previous night. "I'll simply follow the chap and apprehend him."

Sure enough at just after five a young man walked down the soi and began to take Daeng's tuk-tuk. At that point Bob realised that Daeng had left the key in the ignition. Bob wanted to shout out, Good Lord, man! but he satisfied himself by muttering it under his breath. Within a minute Bob had realised the error in his simple plan. The tuk-tuk sped off down the soi as Bob attempted to follow at a quick walking pace while trying to tuck into the side so he couldn't be observed. He saw the back lights of the vehicle as it turned right fifty metres or so down the small road. Bob opened his notebook and added to his case notes.

5:15am tuk-tuk taken. Affirmative. Turned right at end of soi 5:17am. Pursuit ended.

ELEVEN

Marjorie had been particularly wound up by the most recent BWBLS meeting. Gladys's throw away comment was anything but a casual remark, in her opinion.

"Typically passive aggressive of her. I care as much about the environment as the next man," she ranted away to her driver, Sapong, as he drove her to the Central Embassy shopping mall. Sapong spoke solid English, enough for the tasks required of him, but not enough for him to fully engage with Marjorie's ranting. He had learnt the art of being a sounding board and did a lot of nodding or answering in the affirmative. "Yes, yes, Miss Marjorie," or when in his native tongue, "khrap pom, khun Marjorie."

She had been further wound up when, having won the morning's bridge game she had to endure the horrendous Linda Taylor loudly singing Gladys's praises yet again. "It's such a shame Gladys doesn't play bridge any more. She could teach us all a thing or two."

Gladys smiled. "I'm far too old for that, Linda, darling, but aren't you sweet. Reading the Bangkok Post letter page is enough for me." Gladys had a twinkle in her eye as she spoke.

On that day she'd had another of her long letters published, in her role as chair of the board of the Suprawongse Education Trust. It was such a lengthy letter it almost passed for an editorial, but the paper was more than happy to give up space for Khunying Gladys. This letter was a focus on educational progress in Thailand.

There followed twenty minutes of the women all fawning over Gladys as she explained the programmes her foundation were putting in place and the sterling work they were doing to help children of Burmese and Cambodian labourers go to school. Linda turned to Marjorie and icily spoke, "Isn't her energy remarkable?"

"I give money to charity, Sapong!" she continued with her rant.

"Yes you good lady, na khrap. Help many people alway."

"I do, Sapong, I do!"

She continued muttering, mainly to herself really. "Why do they love Gladys so much, why?" "She nice old lady. Alway smile. So nice."

"Oh dear, Sapong. You can be terribly naïve at times, you really can."

Sapong drove into the basement car park at the Central Embassy Mall. Marjorie gave him two hundred baht to get himself some lunch and she told him she would text when she was ready to leave. She'd be at least two hours.

Sapong and his wife Nitarat had been working for

the Dubshotts for twenty years, since they were a young couple with two young children. Nitarat was a cook and housekeeper while Sapong worked as a driver, handyman, and anything else that was needed. The Dubshotts had been wonderful employers. Despite Marjorie's misguided comments and at times what appeared her casual racism, she, along with Humphrey, had been incredibly generous. They paid Sapong and Nitarat salaries above the market rate, but far more than that they had provided them with accommodation and the Dubshotts had funded both their sons' education through one of Thailand's best schools. At first Sapong was very unsure of the move. How would their boys, eight and six years old at the time, cope with an environment with so many hi-so Thai people. It was quite something. Parents at the school included government ministers, high ranking military officials, business leaders and even at times film actors. That world was certainly not reachable for the sons of a driver and cook. Humphrey Dubshott had noticed something in the boys. He realised that they were certainly smart enough to cope with the demands of a good school and he had pulled a few strings through contacts at the British Embassy to see to it. Pie and Arm had thrived there. As teenagers they had gone through patches of embarrassment at the difference between their lives and that of their friends, but they had managed to get over that. They realised how hard their parents had worked and that everything they did was for the two of them. In fact their parents felt even more uncomfortable going to any school function than the boys ever had, but they didn't shy away from any important events for their kids. Both boys had excelled academically and inevitably climbed socially in a way that would otherwise have been unimaginable. However, there were still occasions where they felt like outsiders from their social group. After finishing their high school lives, both had studied at Thammasat University, again with the financial support of Humphrey and Marjorie. Pie had followed a career path in management consultancy and was working in Bangkok, for one of the world's major firms. Arm had followed a more 'glamorous' path and could currently be found presenting a zany and ludicrous light entertainment programme on Thai TV, complete with sound effects; the boings and crashes that Thais found so hilarious. He was something of a C-list celebrity but his stock was rising. That he was an openly gay man was hardly an interest story on Thai TV, but as the son of a driver from a poor farming background who had risen to the top he most certainly was. He was lauded as proof of the changes in Thailand – it wasn't all about the urban elites. Anyone could rise to the top in twenty-first century Thailand, they said. Of course the truth was somewhat different. Scratch beneath the surface and one could quickly find that Arm and Pie were the exception that proved the rule.

In the industry Nong Arm had been the subject of much bitching and gossiping as for eighteen months he was dating a TV executive some twenty-five years his senior. They'd broken up and the gossipers had cynically claimed Arm had dumped the older man once he established himself in his TV career. Again, the opposite was true. Arm had been the one who was unceremoniously dumped just when he felt they were settled and thinking about a lifetime together.

Arm was devastated by the break-up. However, this was something you would never be able to tell from his impossibly over-happy TV persona.

Sapong blended in as he ate his noodles with fish balls on the side soi close to the fancy mall. No one could imagine this quiet unassuming fifty-two-year-old man was the father of 'Nong Arm' from the TV. Arm and Pie had wanted their parents to retire now that they could afford to support them, but Sapong had explained to the boys that you don't just abandon people who have done so much for you. Neither son really understood, but they certainly admired their parents. Sapong and Nitarat found their boys' lives hard to fathom. They were so different from anything they had ever experienced or even imagined, but they were incredibly proud. Nitarat still got tearful when she saw her younger son on TV, such was her disbelief at how their lives had panned out.

TWELVE

Bob hatched what he thought was a genius plan. He would stake out the tuk-tuk thief step by step. He now knew that the guy turned right about fifty to one hundred metres down the road, so the next time he would simply settle himself in at that corner to see where the thief went next. It might take him a few days but Bob expressed to Susie, "It's the sort of genius that separates investigators like The Lowe from mere mortals, Suze."

Susie was not entirely convinced. She sat and pondered for a moment before she made what she felt was an obvious suggestion.

"Why don't you just go on a bicycle, Bob?"

"No, no, Suze, oh good Lord. Dearie me, the naivety. When one is on what we privates call a stakeout, one must just blend in." Bob chuckled in the most patronising of ways.

"But at five am with a dark T-shirt on no one is going to notice you at all, come on, Bob, surely?" Susie confidently declared.

"Just not possible, Suze, besides I don't have a bike," Bob continued in a similar vein.

"Well, you could borrow mine. No probs."

"Bob Lowe PI, on a woman's bike! Tish! Utter nonsense!"

"Well, it's not actually a woman's bike."

"Susie, will you just leave the complex world of private investigations to the experts, namely ME!" Bob now took on a frustrated and angry tone. Susie rolled her eyes "Whatever, Bob."

Bob's anger at such an innocuous point, seemed odd but he had bad memories of attempts to use a bicycle, many miserable and humiliating failed attempts. He had of course tried to learn as a child, but the balance and coordination required was totally beyond him. His parents didn't understand how it was possible for someone to find it so unfathomably difficult even with stabiliser wheels attached. But young Bob just couldn't do it, toppling over at the merest sight of an obstacle. His parents had quietly given up trying to teach him and the small bike was tucked away in the back of the garage.

When he was in his early twenties a girlfriend suggested a few days' cycling holiday in Kent, the 'Garden of England'. He was excited by the idea and had just assumed that with all the years that had passed he would now be able to ride a bike; after all, everyone else could. It stood to reason that he would not have any problems. The reality proved a little different. They had packed their brand-new bikes onto the train before disembarking at a station just outside the Kent county border. Bob's first foray on the bike was quite remarkable. He had barely pushed his foot on the pedal and he was lying in the gutter at the side of the road.

"Damn and blast! Think my shoe got caught. Unbelievable, right, off we go now." Bob shrugged off his failure but the second attempt, while slightly better, saw him cycle right into the middle of the road and into the side of a slow-moving car, with a now bewildered elderly driver. Bob tried two more times with even less success. The girlfriend dumped him then and there on the side of the road and cycled off into the horizon. Bob was left with bruises and scrapes and re-boarding a train back to London. He had never bothered to try and cycle again.

Bob didn't speak to Susie again that evening and left early next morning to continue his stake-out of the tuk-tuk thief. He waited at the street corner with a view of Daeng's house. Right on time again the tuk-tuk thief did his thing. Bob was tucked in beside a car sipping his 7-Eleven cappuccino and waiting patiently. The tuk-tuk turned right as expected and then instantly swung a left just a few yards further ahead. Bob followed at a swift walking pace and to his surprise saw the tuk-tuk parked up by a house just down the road. He waited, hidden by a shrub and took some notes. Bob's notes were much like his speaking, *Remarkable business, TT parked up outside a house. Waiting.*

A few minutes later the man emerged with an older woman and began to load the tuk-tuk with various bags and containers. Bob wasn't able to get any clear view of what they were but he started to wonder if he had stumbled upon something big. He felt a tingling down his spine, a mixture of fear and excitement. He scribbled in his notes. *Possible drug deal?*

Bob had recently been watching the hit TV series *Breaking Bad* and he wondered if this woman in her late fifties had done similar and got some ideas from that. Just what was in those bags. Yaba pills? Cocaine? Ya ice – the local name for crystal methamphetamine. Minutes later the man sped off with the stash and turned right at the end of the road back towards the main Silom Road. The woman walked slowly back into the house. Bangkok never ceased to amaze Bob, here he was watching this middle-aged Thai woman who was possibly a drug kingpin. Bob would set himself up at the next corner next time, although he also considered that this house might need some careful watching. No doubt unsavoury characters would be coming and going all times of the day and night, taking delivery of the good stuff from this unassuming woman.

Bob was very pleased with his efforts and laughed inside at Susie's questioning of his methods. He wondered if he might write a book 'Bob Lowe's step by step stakeouts – for the non-driving, non-cycling private investigator'. A wordy title perhaps but he could work on that.

THIRTEEN

Avi sat in the same bar, and looked at Bob Lowe's business card. After a couple of beers he had texted Lowe a few nights previous. Now he was wondering what on earth he'd been thinking. Employing a private investigator in Bangkok to find a friend he last saw in Tokyo in 1983. He took a big swig of his beer and looked wistfully into space.

"You thinking maak maak again, Avi!" Mint interrupted him.

"I'm remembering an old friend, Mint." Avi felt a tear well in his eyes. Mint didn't notice, she was too busy as the bar was pretty full.

Avi remembered the last time he saw Mo Razzaq, and he was still racked with guilt.

Tensions had begun to appear in the relationship in the early '80s if Avi was honest. By 1982 they had more arguments and disputes than good times. But for a while it helped their disco skills, when they were dancing in tandem. Both were so determined to outdo the other that their focus was constant. They never flinched, their scores were getting better and better as their friendship disintegrated. As they approached the 1983 World Championships in Tokyo they had serious hopes of winning the disco pairs, and both would be in with a shout of winning the blue ribbon of disco – the all-around disco champion. Truth was Mo had slowly stolen a march on Avi and had been consistently a top three performer in solo competitions for the previous year, while Avi had rare forays into the top ten. His bust-up with Mohammed was beginning to strain his own solo dancing.

Thinking back now, and even at the time, Avi found it hard to understand why he suddenly began to dislike Mo. He remembered at one time thinking he hated him. Some thirty-five years later and he had no idea at all why. He remembered what he did though, he'd had to live with that shame. That look on Mo's face was permanently etched in Avi's mind. "Why Avi? Why?" With tears streaming down his face Avi had left the venue and taken the first flight to Tel Aviv. He had never spoken with Mo again. In the pre-internet age it was pretty simple to lose contact with someone living in another country.

He held Bob Lowe's card in his hand, having pulled it from the menu in the bar. Mint noticed

"You know Bob na?"

"No, no, Mint, but maybe I speak with him."

"That him na, sit there always. He like drink beer." Mint pointed to a tall and scruffy chap sitting at the front of the bar gazing out to Soi Nana. Avi jigged his way over to Bob's table.

"Bob Lowe, I believe. Mint said."

"Ah the delightful Mint, where is the old girl. Ah, Mint!" Bob bellowed across the bar and waved.

"Sorry. Yes Bob Lowe indeed. Lowe by name... no hang on that doesn't work does it. Good Lord. Let's start again. Yes, I am Bob!"

"Hi, Bob, I'm Avi. I sent you a LINE message the other day, about a case I may have for you, well I thought I had a case for you, but now I'm not so sure if it's a good idea to go down this path."

"Aha. You leave that to me, Mr Avi. Customer's remorse we call that in the trade, but give me the details and I'll let you know if I can sort you out. No job too small, old boy."

"Well this job is rather big." Avi meekly added.

There was a longish pause and Bob with his improving social skills realised Avi wasn't ready to talk. He tried to change the conversation, gesturing with his hand to the soi.

"Remarkable soi this, isn't it? A decade plus for me and it never ceases to amaze."

Avi looked out wistfully and pondered Bob's words.

"Yes, I suppose it is in its own way, it's certainly an odd place. Perhaps that's why I love just relaxing out here."

"It is that. It is that," added Bob, not quite sure where this conversation was heading. "For many people the beautiful ladies help." Bob raised an eyebrow and flicked his head towards some of the young girls working in the bar.

"Yes, yes, of course, not really for me though."

"No, of course not *you*. Ho ho. Wink wink. Nudge nudge. Eh eh. How's your father." Bob had naturally assumed Avi was just being coy or sarcastic or perhaps simply embarrassed.

"Genuinely, Bob. I come here regularly. I drink. I

chat. I 'hang out' as the kids say. But pick up these girls? No. Not for me."

This was a new one on Bob, and he wasn't sure how to proceed. Of course Bob was aware that many people came to Nana to gawp and experience the place, but they weren't regulars. A regular punter in Nana's bars just to drink and chat? Was this really a thing? Bob considered there were surely more straightforward places in town to have a quiet drink.

"Well, of course, the beer can be cheaper here than in other places, you know those fancy hotels, boy they don't half crank up the prices. Shocking stuff, genuinely remarkable."

Bob was desperately fishing for a logical explanation to this Avi character.

"Yes that is true, Bob. Can't say I am really much of a heavy drinker though."

This was already proving a challenging case for Bangkok's newest private investigator and he hadn't even established what the case was yet! Bangkok was always throwing up these bizarre characters and so in that sense Avi was nothing unique, simply by virtue of his apparent uniqueness.

"So, what sort of cases do you take, Bob?" asked Avi, starting to get to the crux of the matter.

"Oh good Lord! What don't I take?! The range is huge, vast really. Obviously I can't say too much, client confidentiality you see, but I deal with all sorts. Stolen tuk-tuks, cheating partners, you name it, Lowe is getting right in amongst it."

"Missing people?" Shielmann enquired.

"Exactly. You're getting it."

"I've lost two things that are very dear to me Bob. Can you find them?"

"If Lowe can, no one can. No hang on, that's not right either. If Lowe can't, no one can. That's it!"

"My dear, dear friend, Mohammed Razzaq. We had an argument. It was my fault. I've not seen him since."

"I see. I see. Well you've come to the right man. I know how to locate people in this fair city, police contacts you see…" Bob tapped his index finger on his nose.

Avi waved Bob's comments away with a dismissive waft of his hand.

"No. I last saw Mo in Tokyo." Avi paused. "In 1983."

Bob spluttered his beer across the table. "Tokyo! 1983! Good Lord, man, that is a challenge."

Avi was starting to hear the lunacy of what he was saying and with a glint in his eye added, "He's from Pakistan."

"Of course he is! Where else?!" hollered Lowe, beginning to wonder if this was some sort of joke. This strange chap in Nana looking for a Pakistani friend he had last seen in Japan over thirty years ago.

"Are you also from Pakistan?" Bob knew this man clearly wasn't Asian but he didn't want to make any assumptions. He'd landed himself in all sorts of hot water with a young British woman for suggesting she was Malaysian when she was in fact British. Frightful business ending with her shouting out that Bob was a typical old-school racist.

"Of course I'm not! Do I look Pakistani?!" Avi was somewhat bemused by this odd question.

"Well, these days you know. Can never be too careful. When is a Pakistani not a Pakistani?"

"Well, when he is not from Pakistan and has never

even been to Pakistan! I'm Swedish."

"Aha, that's more like it. Lots of you Swedes here in Thailand. Marvellous people the Swedes. We have an Ikea here now you know."

Bob was trying to regain a type of composure, in a very Lowesque way.

"… but I was born an Israeli." Avi was having fun now.

"Oh for heaven's sake, man! Are you trying to confuse The Lowe?" Bob retrieved his notebook from the big baggy pockets on the side of his khaki shorts and explained to Avi that he had to take extensive notes on their conversation. Anything Avi said could be a vital clue, Bob explained. Bob began to scribble furiously. Muttering to himself as he did,

"Quite remarkable. Of course I will need full details if you expect me to solve this case. Now who is the second person you said you had lost."

"No, one person. The other thing, well that's a bit more complicated." Avi could see the look of utter confusion on the Brit's face and wondered if this might stop Bob taking the case at all.

"More complicated?! Heavens forfend, man! How much more complicated can you possibly get?"

"Disco, Bob, disco."

"Disco?" Bob didn't know how he was meant to respond.

"Where is my love of disco, Bob? The glamour. The spandex. The 1970s. Ahh disco…"

"Now look here! I don't know what's going on. A person I can find. But your love of disco. Well, what? What on earth do you expect me to do?" Bob took a large swig of his beer and waved to Mint "We'll be needing more of these, young Mint." As he stretched his arm across the table to attract Mint's attention he casually knocked over Avi's bottle."

"Oh good Lord! Mint!"

Avi was enjoying the whole experience of drinking with this rather peculiar British chap and considered that maybe this was exactly the sort of eccentric lunatic he needed to meet.

"Yes it is quite the conundrum, Bob, but don't you think the bars of Nana are the perfect place for a disco revival?"

Bob let the words swirl around his head and began to picture himself in spandex dancing to a Bee Gees' classic. Dancing had never been a strength of Bob's due to his astonishing lack of coordination but after eight pints or so he'd always been game to give it a go.

Bob and Avi continued to chat and found they got on well. Avi suggested they should meet again to go into all the details about the complex history of his dancing days with Mo Razzaq. After another thirty minutes or so, Avi decided to get a taxi home and leave Bob with his own thoughts.

"One more?" enquired Mint. She already knew the answer, she'd been playing out this routine with Bob for years.

"Go on then, Mint, you rascal you!"

"Bob not want to drink with new girl?" Mint had noticed it had been quite a while since Bob had looked for company.

"No, no. Not for me, Mint, just another beer is quite enough!"

Bob sat back, slightly confused. Was he actually a reformed character? Was he actually becoming a fully-fledged private investigator?

FOURTEEN

The Central Embassy Mall had eventually become one of Marjorie's favourite places to mill about town; she'd tend to go there at least once a week either to meet friends for lunch or coffee, or sometimes just to window shop. Initially she had been adamant that she was going to boycott the mall as she felt the British government should not be cashing in on land that had been given to them. It wasn't even clear that her understanding of the history was correct, as most sources pointed to the British buying the land in the 1920s from Nai Lert, considered one of Thailand's first property developers. However, Marjorie had read an article that stated the land had been donated to the British, and such was her bitterness at how she had been usurped and forgotten by the British Diplomatic Service after the death of Humphrey, that she decided this was a story she would believe. She would start to rant to all and sundry how the embassy had lost its way since Humphrey left, and how British government cuts were now impacting on the diplomatic service and it was an outrage.

Her marriage to Humphrey had been a difficult one. Marjorie openly admitted in older age that she had married Humphrey purely for social climbing and the glamour of his role. An ambassador's wife, as she was eventually to become, meant something. She felt it had all been worth it. People respected her. Doors opened for her, both literally and metaphorically. She had no physical relationship with Humphrey prior to marriage, which she put down to Humphrey being a bit of a prude and not embracing the attitudes of the 1960s. The wedding night was a disaster. She had assumed that would be the time when their physical relationship would begin and their marriage would be consummated. It was the first time she saw her husband naked. They were staying in a delightful rural hotel in Cheshire, not far from his family estate. Humphrey had stumbled into their bedroom drunk and naked muttering, "I suppose we'd better do this then, tradition and all that." He had been totally unable to perform and had been utterly clueless about what he should be doing. Marjorie spent twenty-five minutes trying to get him going, but to no avail. "Too much bloody champagne no doubt," were the last words he said before falling asleep. They tried again a few weeks later, with a greater degree of success, although from Marjorie's perspective it was pretty unsatisfactory. So their marriage became thus; physical intimacy happened about two or three times a year as Marjorie desperately wanted to have a baby. Eventually she accepted this was unlikely to happen and she threw herself into the role of a diplomat's wife with great gusto when Humphrey got his first overseas placement in Kenya in the 1970s. Being

British High Commissioner in the relatively newly independent country was quite a challenge but with Marjorie by his side the couple made it a resounding success.

She began to assume Humphrey must be a closet homosexual; *What a dreadfully dull cliché* she would write in her diary as she noticed an array of attractive young Kenyan men always around her husband both at work and at home. The truth was more complex. Eventually she confronted Humphrey in a blazing row and she told him that it was rather pathetic in these times that he couldn't admit who he was. She knew it was unfair, but it just came out in the heat of the moment. Whilst it was true by that era there were a few gay men in some aspects of public life and the 1960s had all been about free love and sexual experimentation, there were still very few *out* gay men and certainly not in the diplomatic service.

Humphrey was honest with her. He told her that he too had wondered if he was that way inclined, as he did indeed see the beauty in some of the young men who worked for him, but the idea of anything more than appreciating their beauty appalled him. He broke down in tears "What's wrong with me?"

Marjorie was shocked. This sort of emotion was something that she had never seen from her husband. She felt pity for him at that moment and over the following twelve months from that conversation they established a way to make their marriage work. Humphrey promised to do his best to give Marjorie a child and publicly she enabled them to play the wonderful diplomatic couple to perfection.

Marjorie sat down in the lounge restaurant at the

Park Hyatt that was attached to the Central Embassy and ordered herself a latte. She had become overrun with feelings of bitterness and anger. After Humphrey's death, from an enormous heart attack on the golf course, she had quickly become an irrelevance. Being the widow of the former ambassador had little distinction and very quickly a new ambassador had arrived; young with a beautiful wife and three children, they were everything that Marjorie had dreamed of from her union with Humphrey. She hated them for it, and the likes of Linda Taylor never missed a chance to speak in Marjorie's earshot about how dynamic the new ambassador was. Yes, Marjorie Dubshott hated the world and, it seemed, everything in it.

Linda strutted her way down the steps towards the café and Marjorie noted that she was attempting to 'power dress' in a sort of business suit that was totally inappropriate for a casual coffee and shopping. She really had no clue.

"Linda!" Marjorie tried not to shout too loud but Linda hadn't noticed her and was walking to the wrong end of the café. Eventually she turned and walked towards the table.

"Ah, Marje, lovely to see you."

"What a delightful jacket, Linda, is it new?" Marjorie sounded almost genuine.

"Just a little thing I had made for me. Do you know Vichai Singh? He's the top tailor in town you know," Linda proudly stated.

"Of course. Humphrey was a regular there." A classic passive aggressive put-down, this time too subtle for Linda to pick up on. Marjorie thought it comical that any woman would go to Vichai Singh.

He was indeed a fantastic tailor, but his specialism was men's suits and shirts.

The two women made idle small talk about the quality of Central Embassy, the coffee at the Park Hyatt and the general state of Bangkok; weather, politics, traffic. Linda eventually changed the subject.

"So, I must confess, Marjorie, I was surprised to get a coffee invite from you. We haven't always really seen eye to eye." Linda tried her best to sound casual and relaxed.

"I know, I know and that's my fault, Linda. I feel I owe you an apology."

"For what, Marjorie?"

"I've never been very welcoming to you and I don't know why..." Marjorie dabbed her eyes with a tissue and looked crestfallen. "Oh, my life really is a mess." The tears began to flow.

"Oh, Marjorie! Whatever's the matter?"

Linda got up and awkwardly tried to give Marjorie a tender and caring rub on the shoulder.

"There, there, my dear. What's wrong?"

After a moment Marjorie composed herself. "I suppose I've always felt a bit jealous of you."

"Me?!" Linda was genuinely stunned but felt a warmth and pride at the unlikely turn of events.

"Yes. You and Simon have such a perfect marriage, lovely children, and you... young and so attractive. Sorry. I really am feeling sorry for myself."

This was truly extraordinary and Linda pondered to herself how life never stopped throwing up these surprises. She should really be careful before she started judging people. She had long assumed Marjorie was just a snobbish evil witch. Yet the truth was, it seemed, that she was a woman in pain. Her life was a mess. They spent a good hour chatting, Marjorie coming clean on her difficult marriage to Humphrey and how she'd felt cast aside as the widow of the ex-ambassador. Linda felt a real empathy and then some guilt. Here was a fellow woman, battling away in a man's world. She felt an unlikely new friendship was forming. They said goodbye with a warm hug and agreed to meet up for dinner sometime soon.

FIFTEEN

Bob wasn't quite sure how to deal with his latest discovery; the old woman and the possible drug boss situation. Should he inform the police? He was suddenly acutely aware that he had entered into the world of investigations and private detection without so much as a clear plan for these sorts of scenarios. "Pull yourself together, Lowe," he barked out loud to himself. He did know one policeman, Khun Pun, who was something of a regular in one of Bob's favourite Nana bars. Bob even had Pun's number stored in his phone, something he was immensely proud of. You had to really be a proper local Bangkoker to have the number of one of the boys in brown available in your phone. He had only used it once.

One drunken night, Bob Lowe had famously challenged Pun to a game of pool, and promptly lost eight games in a row. They had become quite friendly after that, and Pun had been more than happy to intervene that time Bob called him. Bob had been stopped by the police and asked to complete a urine test, with a joint in his hand. Bob who was a sometime heavy smoker, had absent-mindedly pulled a joint out of his cigarette packet, having tucked it there for safekeeping, and brazenly wandered the streets smoking it. A quick phone call to Pun and he had settled the issue. Pun immediately smoothed things over with the police and he even gave Bob some friendly advice to avoid that particular junction for the next few weeks as the police would be there in force looking to drug test and fine for drunken behaviour.

Bob considered his options and came to the conclusion that it was too soon to involve the police. He gave Pat a call and asked if she was free for dinner.

"Wow! Twice in such a short time, I am honoured, Bob!" Pat giggled.

"Yes, yes, Nong Pat, dinner on me of course, I need your advice on a case."

"Ooh, serious, na. Maybe Pat can be your junior detective. Fifty thousand baht a month okay, Bob ka?" Pat had always enjoyed teasing Bob.

"Easy, tiger! It's still early days, I'm not employing just yet, but who knows, in future…"

"Ha ha, Bob, just joking, na ka! See you later."

Bob hung up the phone and pondered their exchange. He considered out loud, "Curious, is Pat smitten with The Lowe at last?"

With multiple cases, Bob had started to realise that his small, cheap notepads were not sufficient for the copious and complex notes he needed to be writing and made a trip to B2S, one of Bangkok's best stationery supply shops, to purchase something more befitting of someone now in law enforcement. He saw an attractive display of colourful leather-bound journals that looked ideal. He picked one that was about A5 size, perfect for his needs. He turned to the back to check the price, just over one thousand baht.

"Remarkable!" exclaimed Bob, at a volume loud enough to attract the attention of anyone in the shop at the time.

"Utterly remarkable. Simply impossible."

He summoned over a member of staff to fix what he was sure was an obvious error.

"This, phit na khrap?" He expected the lady to have a look and simply confirm that yes it was indeed a mistake.

"Mai phit ka." She nervously replied that there was no mistake.

"You lot must think I was born yesterday! Yesterday! Re-mark-able!"

Bob searched the shop and found an array of cheaper school-style exercise books, some spiral bound in the one-hundred-baht price range. They didn't have the leather or the sophisticated elasticated system to keep it neatly closed, but Bob was a step ahead there. He also bought himself a large bag of rubber bands which would serve that purpose perfectly. As he paid he was determined to get the final word.

"You'll never scam The Lowe!"

He pointed at the exercise book and then the rubber bands and then gesticulated towards the fancy leather-bound journals and shouted "Same, same! Same, same!"

As he stomped out the store the shop assistant muttered "not same" and giggled.

Bob had arranged to meet Pat at the Emporium

Mall so that they could choose from one of the many eating options either in Emporium or Emquartier. He couldn't wait to tell Pat how he had saved a fortune on his notebooks.

As usual Pat looked the figure of relaxed and friendly beauty, that was how Bob had always considered her. She wasn't a classic beauty but she had an incredible warmth.

"You're looking as wonderful as ever, Nong Pat."

"Oh, Bob, want marry me, na?" Pat laughed and immediately realised it was too much for poor Bob who went bright red in the face.

"The Lowe, married?! Good Lord! I mean, er... what?"

"Just joke, Bob. I know I much too old for you!" Pat laughed and immediately changed the topic.

"Let's go for Japanese, I feel like sushi."

"As the lady doth request."

As they walked into Emquartier, Bob continued to wonder if Pat *was* actually attracted to him. Was it possible? These confounded jokes she kept making were very confusing. Were they jokes?

He cast his mind back to a dream he'd once had when they had worked together. Pat was in the store cupboard of the admin office at the language school and Bob had wandered in looking for her. "Pat, are you here? I need help with the photocopier." Bob was forever finding the machine jammed on him and so this aspect of the dream was very believable.

"In here, Bob," Pat called from the cupboard. As Bob walked in he saw Pat lying naked on a pile of books. "I love you, Bob. I want you. I need you."

Bob woke up at that point and was furious as he wanted the dream to continue. The following week at school he walked into the admin office, looking for Pat. As in the dream she called him from the store cupboard. Bob panicked, sweat pouring down his face. He loosened his collar. He slowly walked towards the door and opened it with trepidation.

"Hi, Bob, could you get that box down for me?"

Bob sighed. His shoulders slumped. For just a few seconds he was living the dream, but reality had once again kicked in all too soon. That had been the closest he had actually got to thinking that he and Pat could actually be a thing. Now he couldn't see any possible way forward with Pat, romantically speaking. The irony of Bob's 'successes' with the women in Bangkok had left him short of confidence and totally incapable of approaching a woman in a traditional way. It hadn't always been like this. As a younger man, working in London, he'd happily approach a woman in a bar and ask to buy her a drink, or simply spark up a conversation. He'd dated women throughout his twenties. Sometimes as he looked back he tried to convince himself that nothing had changed. Back then he was a young investment banker, flush with cash. Wasn't the principle just exactly the same? Maybe even those women were attracted by his job and perceived wealth as opposed to his personality and sparkling conversation. He then scolded himself for this line of thought. "New Lowe, less misogynist more feminist."

Bob and Pat sat down at a favourite sushi restaurant. She ordered for them both.

"You're the expert, Nong Pat."

"Oh I see! Asian woman must know all about Sushi. I'm Thai, not Japanese!"

"Yes, very droll." On this occasion Bob was wise

to Pat's gentle ribbing. Pat demonstrated how to mix the wasabi paste with soy sauce.

"Honestly! I do not need lessons. The Lowe is an international man." Bob stirred in much too much wasabi and then rather ham-fisted with the chopsticks he dropped a piece of sushi into the dipping sauce. He fished it out with his hands; "confounded cheap chopsticks, not up to the job" and stuffed the sushi into his mouth, with attached extra lump of wasabi that had not been properly mixed in. "Oh good Lord! Spicy! Aaah!"

Pat just glanced up. "International man, lor?"

SIXTEEN

Police Sergeant Apichit Wuttiwattana (Pun to his friends) was something of a Nana fixture. Not because he was a boozing womaniser – although Pun had always enjoyed a few beers he had never been unfaithful to his wife of nearly twenty years – but because he had been the senior law enforcement officer working Soi Nana for just over five years. He'd seen it all, and more. The job had of course proved to be very profitable for him. The system of bribes, payoffs, and commission payments to junior officers was extremely complex but the long and short of it was that Pun made a small fortune from these streets. This was a way of policing that just worked in Thailand and it certainly worked for Apichit Wuttiwattana. Pun felt that the Thai system, rather the unofficial Thai system, ensured that small issues could be dealt with quickly and effectively. In Europe even minor traffic offences might result in yards of paperwork; fines being administered, people appealing, letters and emails being sent back and forth. Pun had heard all about it and found the very notion of such a lengthy administrative process utterly ludicrous.

Pun would see what he wanted to see, or to be more accurate he would see what he felt he *needed* to see. His main aim was to ensure that the goings on in Nana were confined to harmless consensual fun, and a bit of escapism. Did it really matter if every establishment obeyed the letter of the law when it came to the licensing of booze? No, of course it didn't. For a few thousand baht a week from each bar, the police would officially turn a blind eye. His own personal moral and ethical code was important to Pun. There were lines that he would never cross, regardless of any potential financial rewards. Not all police officers shared his own unique attitude but Pun was one hundred per cent sure he was right, always. Did a young foreigner really need to go to prison for possession of a joint or a small amount of something that little bit stronger? Pun felt that for such a misdemeanour when someone was obviously using for purely recreational purposes, that ten to twenty thousand baht and a warning was more than adequate. He was proud of how 'his' bars operated. There were areas in Bangkok where boys and girls under the age of eighteen worked, almost openly, in bars and massage parlours and were of course available for hire. Not in any of the bars in Pun's area of Soi Nana. Unheard of. There was a strong moral contract between Pun and the mamasans who managed the bars that was never broken.

Pun lived a life that simply couldn't be achieved on his official salary, even as a high-ranking officer. His family enjoyed one or two holidays a year to expensive locations (they had been skiing in Switzerland last year), and his daughter attended an expensive international school in Bangkok. Some of the boys in her class had googled the salary of a policeman and joked with Mae about how her dad could be so rich when his salary was apparently so low. Mae tried to laugh it off. She had asked her dad once and he gave what she felt was a perfectly acceptable explanation. Firstly, he claimed that the kids in her school shouldn't be believing anything they read online. "Police salaries are very complicated, remember I am a senior officer. The Royal Thai Police does not put our salaries on the internet."

That alone did not satisfy Mae, so Pun added, "Don't forget your mother and me make a lot of money from our investments and properties." Mae left it there, not thinking deeper about how they had so many investments and properties! She now had a good response for the kids in school when they tried to mock and imply her dad was part of a corrupt system.

Pun was a solidly-built man, of medium height with a short-cropped hair style. He had managed to just about avoid the bulging gut that was so prevalent among many of Thailand's officers and that had becoming something of a national embarrassment. Sure, Pun was on the chunky side but he could get away with being seen as more muscular than fat, just. It was a close-run thing though and Pun spent many hours in the gym to keep his physique on the right side of the line. He had a warm but wise face, which worked perfectly for him. People always felt at ease in his company, but no one thought they could out think him and he was very skilled at getting people to open up and talk, often even to confess to their crimes. These days he didn't spend as much time on the street as he used to. He had a core of good junior officers who could be relied upon to deliver his method of policing, though he did feel that it was important he visited Nana often enough to retain his visible presence. When it came to handling the regular payments from bars, he left that to his trusted disciples. Yes, Khun Pun ran a tight, well-oiled ship. His role was to stroll around, chat with those in the know (usually the mamasans of Nana's bars) and keep abreast of any important issues. That was the best way to pick up on the gossip and in particular who the main drug dealers were for example. He wandered into Mints bar, and sat down at a table near the back, as he always did. The waitress greeted him extremely politely wai-ing him appropriately and asking him to let her know as soon as he was ready to order something. She knew him well from previous visits. Pun nodded.

Mint approached him within a couple of minutes and they exchanged the usual pleasantries before she asked, "Hamburger with extra bacon and cheese?"

"You know me well, Khun Mint."

Mint barked the order to one of the other waitresses for show, she wanted Pun to know she considered his order a priority. She was a skilled operator and knew how to keep the business running smoothly. Pun never paid for food or a drink, another perk of the job.

Pun picked up Bob Lowe's shabby business card from the table display. "Is this something I need to know about?"

"I don't think so. You know Bob, tall scruffy

farang guy who drinks here often."

"Oh, English Bob? The pool hustler?!" Pun bellowed a deep laugh.

Mint explained that as far as she could work out Bob had a few random clients and wasn't doing much of any interest.

"I'll give him a call, we could help each other, and maybe I'll challenge him on the pool table again! Keep me posted."

"Of course, Pun, of course."

The kitchen had prepared an extra-large portion of fries for their VIP and when the plate with the juicy burger oozing cheese and bacon strips, was placed in front of Pun he smiled but sighed as well.

"This will need extra time in the gym!"

"You're looking as fit as ever, Pun." Mint told him, genuinely. This wasn't an insincere bar girl line.

"You're too kind, Mint."

With that, Mint left him to eat, letting him know to shout if he needed anything. She knew Pun liked to eat his food in peace and couldn't stand someone standing over him chatting while the grease of a burger began to drip down his chin.

Pun tucked heartily into his burger and surveyed the scene. It was very early in the evening and Mints wasn't busy. He very rarely had any issues in this bar. Mint had been effectively running the place for some years and she was something of an expert. Her girls worked hard and there was rarely a cross word between customers and bar girls, or between the girls themselves; which was sometimes a problem in other bars. He observed two guys playing pool. To his finely tuned eye and ear they seemed to be Australians. Both were dressed in shorts, 'wife-beater' tops with a Thai beer logo, and flip-flops. He took an instant dislike to this sort of character. "Why are they dressed for the beach?" he'd often ask his colleagues. He felt his instant judgement was quickly proved justified when one of the guys rather aggressively shouted out that he needed more beer. It seemed he wasn't happy with the service, no one had noticed that his beer was finished. Pun gave a look of utter disdain, before getting up and walking over to the pair.

"Problem here?" Pun had perfected a dismissive, angry cop role from watching movies.

"Nah, mate. These chicks are just slow with my beer." Both men laughed.

Pun couldn't believe the brass neck of these two, laughing like this.

"You like this bar?" Pun increased the amount of sinister in his tone to try and get a message across.

"Yeh it's ok, mate." The taller Aussie spoke, this time with a bit more caution in his voice.

"These girls work hard. You show respect, or you leave. Or you come to the police station with me."

Both men apologised profusely.

"One warning. From me, only one warning. Remember."

With that, Pun strolled back across the bar, gave a small nod of recognition and thanks to Mint and left to continue with his rounds.

SEVENTEEN

Bob was continuing to find it hard to juggle his caseload and was already becoming acutely aware that this business was not as simple as he'd previously thought. He had neglected Pim and Brian, so he sent them some holding texts.

Pim, let's meet up soon to discuss updates to the case. All is going well. Lowe is on it.

By meeting Pim he would effectively be working on the case for Brian, and vice versa when he met Brian. A wonderful situation. This was slick stuff, in his mind. He wondered if he could work out this sort of scenario for all his cases, before quickly realising that to try and engineer such a muddle was both dangerous and foolhardy.

He sat at his laptop and googled *Mohammed Razzak*, over four million hits. This wasn't going to be easy. Bob tried to refine his search but his internet skills were slightly lacking and he got near as nowhere. In his mind he thought he might just find a direct link to a homepage about former disco sensation Mo Razzak, complete with an email contact. He wondered if the Pakistan embassy might be able to help. But his information was very limited. He needed to try and get more details from Avi. Bob knew that great private investigators could find one little seemingly insignificant detail that would ultimately become the key to cracking the whole case. Could he train his mind? He pondered. He made a mental note to read some Hercule Poirot mysteries, perhaps that would get his brain onto the right path.

As for the other part of that case, helping Avi rediscover his love of disco, well Bob was somewhat bemused by this. He wondered if he should add 'therapist' or 'life coach' to his business card. The idea was hilarious. A forty-something washed-up Bangkok expat giving people help in sorting out their lives! You couldn't make this up. Only in Bangkok.

"Remarkable," Bob uttered out loud, as he tended to do.

However he did have some ideas about how he could help Avi and he had already run some of them by the ever-reliable Pat. Bob Lowe, PI, Life Coach, Event Promoter. What else could he add to his repertoire? He knew enough of the mamasans in town who he thought he could convince to arrange special disco appearances from the former great Avi Shielmann. 'For one night only' he could use that line repeatedly in different bars around town. "Classic marketing trick, Lowe," he bellowed.

He began to list possible venues, focusing on the ones where he had a good rapport with the staff. They would easily accommodate his wishes. He had found some YouTube videos from the old 'World Disco Championship' days, one with Avi representing

Israel. Avi was quite a dancer, it had to be said. He had also perfected a big cheesy grin as he strutted his moves. On one of the videos Bob was fortunate enough to see Mo Razzaq. Razzaq! With a Q!

"Aha! Gotcha!" Bob again shouted to an empty room.

He then got distracted watching cricket videos as his Mo Razzaq searches brought up some links to the Pakistani cricket star, Abdul Razzaq, and before long Bob was immersed watching videos of some of his favourite cricketers from the sub-continent.

"Wonderful!"

"Remarkable!"

"Wristy!"

Bob then laid back on his sofa and slipped into a typical Lowe daydream. He imagined himself in his late forties, part of an intrepid group of Thai cricketers foraging their way in the one-day game. 'Bob Lowe, swashbuckling middle order bat, and tricky wrist spinner.'

The most amusing thing about Bob's daydreams was that even they had a hint of tragedy or near-misses. In one, he was bravely flogging the Aussies all over the ground; the quickest century in one-day cricket history, before he was agonisingly run out with victory in sight.

Bob realised he was running late for his meeting with Pim and launched himself off the sofa, leaving behind a pool of sweat that had formed on the cheap faux-leather covering. He texted Pim to explain he'd be a little late due to a complex case issue. Bob had arranged to meet Pim once again at Coffee Corner. He liked the continuity, also it helped his brain to focus on the correct case. He had a terrible fear of slipping up while working for both Pim and Brian.

"Pim, my dear. Sabai dii mai khrap?" Bob asked Pim how she was in his best Thai.

"I'm fine. How are you?" Pim spoke nervously.

"Couldn't be better, young Pim. Now, I've been exceedingly busy on your case, putting in the hours, approaching it from different angles." He was increasingly confident in his bullshit now.

"Brian, he have many gik chai mai?" Pim got directly to the point. A 'gik' in Thai was effectively a mistress and was an extremely common word. It was also said that for many men, having a gik or two was common practice.

"My initial work phase says no, Pim. But I must add this is early days and I can't be sure yet. I have many different leads and angles to pursue." Bob was talking the talk, for sure.

"That mean what?" Pim wanted this put more simply.

"Well, Pim. He does drink a lot around Nana with work friends, quite regularly. My contacts are monitoring and so far we have no evidence of him 'offing' or 'bar-fining' anyone."

"That good. I worry much."

"Yes, dear Pim, I can see this must be a worry. Now I do have to ask you some difficult questions. One doesn't like to, but this is very much part of the job, as they say." Bob was ready to machete in and work on the other side of the case. Pim was able to predict what Bob wanted to ask.

"You think I work same bar girl, alway. Same many time before?" Pim was able to make herself understood by Bob who was fluent in bar girl English. Another of Bob's hare-brained schemes was to try and make a Bar Girl English to English dictionary. He had even once begun scrawling down words but he got himself all muddled with the phonetics and thought it would need to be an audio dictionary, and then gave up.

"Well yes, Pim, I'm sorry to ask, but I must consider all aspects of the case. Complexities, Pim."

"I no go customer. But sometime customer text me. I worry if Brian bad man, I go new man quickly soon."

Bob was beginning to feel real empathy for Pim's position, not a skill that he usually had. He could see Pim's predicament. She desperately wanted security, wanted out of the bar girl scene, but she needed that with a solid and dependable guy.

"One man. He like me many time. My friend think Brian too young."

Bob was listening intently and allowing Pim to talk.

"Usually I think old man very narak. So I wrong choice for Brian. You think I mistake, Khun Bob." Bob was now putting his life-coach hat back on.

"Nong Pim. My dear sweet Pim. This is quite the pickle. Ordinarily I would advise to follow your heart, but you must be aware of the risk. This old man, tell me about him."

Bob spoke in warm calm tones, putting Pim at ease, even if she didn't fully understand.

"He narak. Very old man, near fifty-eight year old. Germany man. Little grey hair only. He visitor to Bangkok many time. Now he say he stay here talod chiwit."

Bob was amused by Pim using the occasional words in Thai but this was one of those expressions he had no problem understanding. Talod chiwit – forever, for the rest of your life. Bob had uttered this in many a conversation with bar girls over the years. In his more cringe worthy moments, he had expressed love for a new fling 'talod chiwit'.

Bob began to move into what he guessed was very unprofessional territory. "You're glowing when you speak of this German chap. Pim, I think you must go and see him. I can help so Brian doesn't find out."

At that Pim dabbed a tear from her eye.

"You nice man, Bob. Why you no have girlfriend?"

"Good question, my dear Pim! Good question!"

Pim paid Bob for the next instalment and Bob began to make very complex notes. He was now advising a client to cheat on her boyfriend who was also a client who suspected his girlfriend was cheating, which she wasn't until perhaps now with the intervention of Bob Lowe PI. This was getting complicated indeed.

Bob realised that what Pim needed was to know that Brian was indeed a 'bad man' so she could feel that leaving him was the right decision. Bob decided he must do all he could to help Pim. He texted Brian.

Brian, old boy, let's catch up for a beet and case update. Bob Lowe here incidentally. Bob Lowe PI (Private investigator).

He then sent another,

*beet.

And another

*beer! For goodness sake. Beer! Drink. Beer!

"Remarkable. Utterly remarkable. Beet." Bob chuckled heartily.

EIGHTEEN

Marjorie suggested a dinner with Linda at one of her favourite Italian restaurants in the city. A wonderful homely authentic restaurant tucked away around the back of Sukhumvit Soi 20. The owner was Giuseppe Carravalli; an Italian man from Rome, who had lived in Bangkok for over thirty years, he didn't cook himself these days, but the restaurant retained its charming Italian feel, and the authentic décor allowed Marjorie to reminisce about holidays in Italy.

Marjorie arrived at seven pm, just before Linda; she prided herself in never being late, even in a city like Bangkok renowned for its horrendous traffic and particularly at this time of day with rush hour rearing its ugly head. Sapong was something of an expert in reading the conditions and knowing every shortcut there was.

"Sapong, I will text you when I am ready to go, get yourself some dinner." She handed Sapong five hundred baht and waved away his protestations. She would usually give him a couple of hundred when he was having to work late like this but she had no change. Sapong knew he had time to walk down the soi to one of his favourite street restaurants on Sukhumvit Soi 33. The little family run restaurant had been open as long as anyone could remember and had never changed at all, even with the slick modernising of the city that had engulfed most areas.

Marjorie settled herself at the table she had specifically picked out and took the liberty of ordering a bottle of Italian white wine. When Linda arrived she told her it was one of the very best from Tuscany.

"Oh, the holidays we used to have in Tuscany." Marjorie always referred to 'we' regardless of whether she was talking in the past or present. She just hadn't got used to the fact that she was alone, even some five years after Humphrey's death.

Linda had never been to 'Casa Roma' and she'd always been keen to try a new restaurant. It had been highly recommended and had started to add a few Thai-Italian fusion dishes which Linda loved. A little extra spice in her Italian food could never be a bad thing.

As they ordered their second bottle the conversation began to get more relaxed and the pair were getting on like old friends.

"Oh, Linda, something awful has happened and I don't know who to tell about it or what to do." Marjorie dived right in.

"Goodness, what's happened, Marjorie?"

"It's about dear, dear Gladys, it's really very awkward. I mean I can't be sure but..."

"What? What is it? Is she okay?"

"Well physically she seems as sharp as ever. But, well over the last few months I think she is losing her mind."

"Gladys!? No! Surely not, she seems the same as ever." Linda was surprised by Marjorie's comments.

"Yes, oh yes, I know, but something has been happening, and it's too awful. I feel terrible making an accusation." Marjorie, it seemed, didn't know quite how to tell Linda whatever it was she needed to say.

"Accusation!? What's happened!?"

"Well. Please, please, do not tell anyone, but I just need to get this weight off my shoulders and ask someone's advice. I am sure Gladys has been stealing cash from the BWBLS funds, both from the account and the weekly cash takings."

"Impossible! Gladys!?" Linda was shocked.

"Oh, I know, I know. I thought the same. For weeks I thought I must be wrong, but there is no other explanation. I've looked into it all."

The two women chatted on and on as the wine flowed. Marjorie explained that she had been to the bank and they had confirmed that the ATM outside Gladys's apartment had been the one used for regular withdrawals. Gladys still retained a bank card, as a sort of honour dating back to when she was treasurer and in particular responsible for the charitable funds.

"She can't possibly be hard up for cash, so the only explanation is that she is losing her marbles. Each week when we put the weekly cash in the tin, while we all focus on our bridge game, well she must be pinching a few thousand then as well. I've definitely observed her acting oddly."

Linda was furious. Something Marjorie had suspected might be her reaction.

"Isn't that just typical? These rich types. They've known nothing but wealth and yet they still decide to suddenly start stealing from the rest of us." Linda's voice took on an acid tone.

"Well none of us are exactly hard up, Linda." Marjorie did her best to diffuse the situation.

"Yes but everyone loves her. How can she behave like this? What a… I'm sorry, I don't mean to be so rude but I am incensed by this! I'll ask Simon what he thinks."

"No! No, we can't tell anyone yet. We don't want Gladys to be humiliated, but well, perhaps you're right. We must do something."

The two women chatted away feverishly and Linda agreed that for the moment it was best to leave this to Marjorie. She repeatedly expressed to Linda that she just wanted to help dear Gladys. They tucked into their meal, Marjorie ordered a delicious ossobuco which was the speciality of Casa Roma. She had tried not to wince when Linda ordered a simple pizza. The pizzas were of course wonderful, with fresh toppings and crispy crust, but in Marjorie's opinion Casa Roma was a few notches up from a mere pizzeria. For dessert Marjorie insisted that they order one tiramisu and one panna cotta to share, and then lectured Linda on the history and origins of both dishes. Linda was enthralled.

"Oh we always love a panna cotta washed down with a chilled, sweet dessert wine." She looked into the restaurant's fresco and imagined herself out in the fresh Italian countryside.

Later in the evening as both ladies enjoyed a limoncello courtesy of Giuseppe himself, Marjorie decided to take a slightly bolder approach where Gladys was concerned.

"I don't want to speak out of turn, but good Lord,

Gladys can be infuriating at times. She's not better than you or me Linda my dear."

As before, Linda felt somewhat flattered at Marjorie seemingly putting Linda on her own level. She was finally being accepted by the upper echelons of Bangkok's expat society. They accepted a refill from Giuseppe and before going their separate ways home they enjoyed some mutual bitching about Khunying Gladys.

NINETEEN

Bob decided the early mornings on his step by step stakeout were too exhausting and felt he would benefit from a couple of days of not having to wake up at four o'clock to manoeuvre himself into position in Silom to view the mysterious tuk-tuk thief. Also, now that he had begun to uncover the truth and this equally mysterious older woman, he felt he needed to spend some time observing *her* actions. He decided to begin a stakeout of her house, starting from a more sensible hour – after eight am. Bob wandered down Soi Convent, popping into the 7-Eleven on the corner on his way. "It's the crème de la crème of the upper echelons of the 7-Eleven world, my dear," he'd explained to his roommate Susie Hoare the previous night. Bob had made a throwaway comment about how he had always enjoyed a visit down to Silom because it allowed him to go to his favourite 7-Eleven and Susie insisted on arguing. Bob was getting fed up with it; she was insistent that all 7-Elevens were fundamentally the same.

"I'm sorry, Susie, but that is the single most ludicrous comment I have heard in my forty plus years on this planet. Really you should be utterly ashamed of yourself." He was genuinely furious.

"For fucks sake, Bob, it's just a 7-Eleven!"

"That is just the sort of nonsensical naivety that makes me question your sanity. How long have you lived in Bangkok?"

"Longer than you!" Susie shouted back fairly aggressively.

"And yet your ignorance of 7-Elevens is plain to see. Right, now would you please leave me alone, I want to sleep!"

"Leave you alone!? This is *my* living room, but okay, Lord Lowe needs his beauty sleep..." With that Susie got up and slammed the door.

Bob had begun to question the rationality of his decision to move in with Susie. Yes, it was enabling him to live rent free, but her attitude was becoming infuriating. She should be honoured to be living with one of Bangkok's most unique private detectives. Yet she was constantly arguing. Bob had quietly stopped mentioning any sort of business partnership as he realised he would find it impossible to work with her.

He chuckled to himself as he examined the items in the vast 7-Eleven at the corner of Convent Road. "Just like any other 7-Eleven. Utter poppycock." A fellow farang gave Bob an odd look as the tall Brit muttered to himself.

He ordered himself a cappuccino and selected a fresh doughnut. "And I am ordering from the freshly baked counter. The mind boggles. It really does," he continued to mutter.

On his way to stakeout the middle-aged drug cartel

boss (as Bob was now casually thinking of the woman), he passed Daeng who was sat outside his house with his friend Nat.

"Sawat dii, Khun Daeng! I working your case"

"Hello, Bob. Tuk-tuk here. One hundred baht again today."

"Marvellous!"

Bob chatted awkwardly with Daeng, checking the meaning of words and using an app on his phone to look up a few more. Bob found out from Daeng that he had a couple of upstairs bedrooms in his house and that Daeng now lived alone.

"I look bedroom for rent?" Bob asked in his finest Thai.

"Here? How much can you pay?" Daeng replied.

"I not rich man. Little money only." Bob was impressed with how well he was being understood.

"Three thousand baht a month?" Daeng offered Bob a deal.

"Interested! Speak next time."

What a fascinating turn of events Bob thought to himself. There he was fed up with Susie Hoare and her arguing and here was the wonderful Daeng needing a lodger. Bob was seriously considering it, but figured he'd need to get Pat to speak with Daeng and clarify that he had correctly understood.

It would be classic Lowe though, he thought. While others lived in fancy high-rise condominiums, Lowe would live on a quiet off-shoot of Soi Pipat among the real Thai people.

"Marvellous!" Lowe declared out loud as he walked off down the soi.

"When life gives you salty fish. You make fish sauce."

Nat looked at Daeng, perplexed.

"You want an odd farang guy living in your house! Have you gone quite mad?"

"Why not? It's boring living alone. Would be interesting. Besides, it will help him work my case." Daeng smiled at Nat. "And three thousand baht is three thousand baht."

Nat nodded. They sat in silence for another five or so minutes before Daeng declared it was time to head off to work.

"Go scam those tourists!" Nat called as he wandered back to his house.

Lowe settled himself in beside a tree on the opposite side of the road, just a few yards down from the drug dealer's house, and proceeded to slurp his coffee and tuck into his doughnut. "Sublime!" he shouted out, then realising he was meant to be quietly poised on a stakeout, he added, "Whoops" in an even louder voice before grimacing to himself, realising his folly. He got out one of his new fancy (but cheap) notepads and flicked through a few pages, adding the odd random comment to help himself.

He started a fresh page and added a title. *Stakeout of ya ice cook's house* then added, *no link to drugs confirmed...but heavily suspected. Bangkok's answer to Heisenberg?*

He made some notes about the house, a typically Thai-style house, with a small front yard that served as a driveway with a very old pickup truck parked there. There was a small wooden table with some rather ornate wooden chairs to one side and a metallic netting-style door covering the front door. It looked like a typically peaceful Thai soi.

After twenty minutes, Bob was alerted to the old woman walking down the soi towards her house. She was carrying one large plastic bag that appeared to be light from the way she was swinging it around. In her other hand she had a fold-up table or chair. She wasn't finding it easy to carry and for a moment Bob considered jumping up to help her, before he remembered his purpose.

She stowed the table/chair in the side by her pickup and then went into the house. He made some basic notes about her appearance. Confirming what he knew from his previous visit; *mid-fifties, handsome, almost striking woman, doesn't look like your normal drug dealer.*

Bob waited patiently and then after another ten minutes a rather shabby young man arrived at her door. "Aha!" Bob couldn't resist the urge to speak out loud, but he had now learnt to whisper. This, he felt was it, obviously a customer coming to pick up some drugs. He looked the type too, slightly swarthy, almost sinister looking. Bob added, *no doubt needs his next hit to get him out of this slump.* Bob continued to write copious notes as he felt eventually he would need to involve the police in this matter. The man chatted for a few minutes and the woman kept gesticulating towards the vehicle. Eventually he walked over to the vehicle, lifted the hood and appeared to tinker inside. Amateur hour, you can't outfox The Lowe, he thought and added to his notes – *drugs almost certainly stashed in engine of vehicle.*

TWENTY

A casual comment by Pat on the recent dinner date had alerted Bob to a fundamental flaw in his BGM (bar girl marketing) policy. With his plan to continue spreading his cards and flyers around the bars of Nana and with him now taking on Brian as a client, why would any Thai woman working in a bar employ him? Of course, Pat was right. If Bob wanted to corner the bar girl market he couldn't possibly have the girls thinking he may also be working for the 'other side' and then potentially stalking and observing them! He started suggesting to Pat that he should add something like "Bar Girls Only!" or "No Farang/Bar Girl cases." Pat managed to politely talk Bob out of this idea, doing well to suppress a laugh in the process. He eventually vowed that he would get word of mouth spread via his network of bar girls, that when it came to matters of the heart he would never ever take a case for a guy who wanted his girlfriend checked up on. If anyone saw him with Brian and realised it was work, he would say it was a boring, business investigation. The complexities of this business had already become endless. Bob added this rule to his 'Lowe PI charter', a sensible list in the back pages of one of his notebooks. Brian would be the first and last client of this ilk, and regardless, he told himself that Brian didn't count as he was obviously on Pim's side in that situation anyway. He could quietly spread it around that actually he once double-crossed a farang. Imagine the cult following he would get. Bob began to daydream, imagining himself walking into a bar and a spontaneous round of applause breaking out. Free drinks, free... he stopped his thoughts there, remembering 'New Lowe' and all that.

He had been surprised and genuinely touched by the way Pim had spoken of this older German man. It was clear that Pim had real feelings for the man and she had been sure that he was 'good man' and that he wasn't into playing the Nana scene and seeing many girls. Bob added his name to the file and decided that if Pim was thinking seriously about this Werner then he would do some pro-bono work for her just to check up on him. Meanwhile he had promised to help her to meet up with him. She had told Bob that Brian was going out to watch football with friends on Saturday evening, so she made plans to meet Werner for dinner. Bob assured Pim he would monitor Brian and inform her if and when he was heading home. He was aware of the bar where Brian usually preferred to watch football, a large open bar near the top of Soi Nana 'Nana Nights' often referred to as NN by regulars. Sure enough, Brian was sat there with a couple of mates. Bob went right over to him "Brian! What a coincidence!"

"Well, we both drink here regularly, Bob, so… no, not really. Join us?"

"Don't mind if I do! What's the live game here tonight?"

Brian informed Bob it was Chelsea vs Newcastle and Bob decided to test his West Ham theory. "Aha. Chelsea fan, Brian?" Bob asked.

"Fuck off, mate! West 'am to the core."

"Of course, the happy hammers." Bob was delighted inside. His football knowledge was seriously limited but he was doing his best to fit in. The biggest roar from the table during the first half was when the scores flashed up and showed that West Ham had scored twice in the first five minutes. "Fuck me. West Ham are getting busy!"

Bob was determined to try and steer the conversation carefully towards the job in hand. "I wouldn't mind getting busy with one of these waitresses." Bob felt slightly uncomfortable talking like this. He hadn't used this sort of language since he'd begun on his path to cleaner living. He was thinking of branding New Lowe as Lowe 2.0.

"Take your pick, Bob mate. Little Jit over there's an absolute fucking beauty. Goes like the fucking clappers"

"Oh yeh? Talking from experience?" Bob was excited now he felt he may be getting close to revealing Brian's philandering.

"Yep. I bar-fined her about a year ago. Fucking magic in the sack. Does whatever you want, mate." Brian seemed to be remembering fondly. Bob decided not to push it and to let Brian continue.

"I don't pick up girls from bars anymore, Bob," Brian calmly stated, before adding, "now I've got a live-in girlfriend."

Bob was momentarily disappointed before Brian added with a glint in his eye, "I go to a couple of massage places near Ratchada, top secret!" He sat back proudly and winked at Bob.

"Nice one, Brian, you gotta keep a few on the go." Bob raised his bottle and tapped it against Brian's. He was celebrating, not Brian's womanising but that in that very moment he had solved his first case. Brian was getting pretty drunk and enjoying the attention. "Well, let's just say, Bob, I know a few girls that will do things that my girlfriend won't do!" His mates roared and laughed.

"Us men have needs!" Bob added, trying to get in on the round of machismo.

"Too fucking right, mate." Brian grinned.

Bob sat there, satisfied but feeling slightly glum. He was saddened for Pim that she had got herself too mixed up with this guy, but on a deeper level he began to reflect on his own years in Bangkok. He felt quite ashamed how he had treated and spoken about some of the women, even if he did have something of a moral compass, in a way that many didn't. He was determined to help Pim in sorting her life out.

As the football match moved into the second half, Bob decided it would be prudent to update Brian on the case.

"Brian, good news. So far your Pim seems to be a good 'un. I've followed her a few times and she has been out with friends, as she told you. Bob slickly flicked through his notebook to give Brian some of the salient details. He hadn't actually followed Pim, he had just trusted that what she said was true.

"I'd like to continue a few more weeks. In my

experience you need to check these things for a slightly longer period of time."

Brian seemed slightly disinterested. "Yeh, no worries, mate. To be honest I suspected Pim was too fucking lazy to be sleeping around."

They both laughed, but inside Bob was seething with rage. He hadn't seen this side of Brian before, and it was clear that with a few drinks inside him and in the company of these friends he didn't want to appear to be someone who gave a shit about his live-in girlfriend. Brian paid another few thousand baht for continuing work and then informed Bob he was off for a 'massage' in Ratchada. He had motioned inverted commas with his fingers and laughed and slapped his mates on the back.

Bob sent Pim an update that Brian was drinking with friends and would be another hour or so for sure.

Getting too late for me now, Pim, off to Bedfordshire.
Pim responded with a confused sticker.

Sleep time! Bob replied. Then feeling he needed to fully clarify he added, *I very tired. I need sleep. In my bed.*

TWENTY ONE

Sapong was strolling down Silom Road, running an errand for Marjorie. She wanted to confirm some details of a flight she had booked with Singapore Airlines and she hated phoning any customer service numbers. She couldn't tolerate the holding on for ages and having to navigate which numbers to press from their menus. That was stressful enough. Language was a whole other issue. While it was true that over the years, the quality of spoken English on such customer service calls had hugely improved, Marjorie still strained to understand. And to confound matters, her Thai simply wasn't good enough for a clear phone conversation. It seemed much easier to send Sapong. He always enjoyed running errands around town, and particularly liked the buzz and energy of Silom Road. All those business types rushing to the office, clasping their iced coffees. It impressed him. This was the sort of life his sons led. There were also a fair number of tourists out on shopping sprees, young university students hanging out in cafés and shopping malls, and of course a smattering of the sorts of random misfits that Thailand seemed to specialise in. One such character staggered past him, a European guy in his thirties with messed up hair and a filthy T-shirt. Sapong wasn't sure if he was drunk, homeless, or both. He seemed to be approaching people asking them for money or something. He looked at Sapong, and Sapong quickly walked by. If needed he could fall back on the 'No English' line. Sapong just didn't get it. Of course he had heard that European countries had plenty of their own problems, but how so many of them ended up like this in Bangkok was beyond his comprehension.

He saw his old friend Daeng leaning back in his tuk-tuk eating some moo ping. It was a while since he had seen Daeng and so he stopped for a chat. Sapong had known Daeng for years; when he first arrived in Bangkok (before working for the Dubshotts) he had lived just near Daeng and Ploy and they had become quite good friends.

"How's things, Daeng?" Sapong tried to surprise his old mate.

"Same as ever." The casual reply was classic of Daeng. None of the 'haven't seen you in ages!' Daeng was just too cool and calm, nothing fazed him.

They chatted cordially and Sapong was fascinated by the story of the British detective who was thinking of moving in with Daeng. It seemed Daeng was also talking about being part of his detective business.

"You've certainly lived the wild life, Daeng!" Sapong had always joked with Daeng about his life meeting thousands of characters driving a tuk-tuk.

He explained to Daeng that his boss, Marjorie,

may be in need of a private detective. He had heard her chatting about some issue with the Bangkok Women's group and thought that she wouldn't want to involve the police. He took a card from Daeng and promised to pass it on to Marjorie. They continued to chat, before Daeng had to leave as a customer approached wanting to go to an address near Wireless Road. Daeng sighed, he was feeling slightly lazy but couldn't really turn down too many fares; he was supposed to be working, after all. He was delighted to have passed on Bob's card again and he knew Bob would be excited to hear he was busy recruiting clients.

Sapong sorted out Marjorie's flight change and then got the Skytrain back to the house. Marjorie always suggested he take the car there, but since he drove most of the time he found it quite refreshing and liberating to be on the train and walking the sois. He had time to catch up with Pie, his elder son. He texted him to ask if he was busy. Pie replied, not directly to the text message but with WhatsApp.

I told u to use this, its free! Pie always wrote his Thai texts in phonetics with Roman letters, 'passa karaoke' as it was known in Thai, karaoke language. His dad could understand it, but he hated it.

And I've told you to text me in Thai! he replied.

They agreed to meet in a Starbucks near Pie's office. Sapong would have preferred a small coffee stall but his kids loved to pay the exorbitant prices of these coffee chains.

They sat down and Sapong immediately tossed a magazine down on the table. "I'm worried about your brother."

The magazine was full of glossy candid celebrity

photos including some of Nong Arm rolling out of bars in the early hours looking the worse for wear. The article strongly hinted that he may have been taking something stronger than just alcohol.

"Dad, you can't believe these magazines. He's fine. A few drinks, a few clubs. He's young and that's the industry he's in." Truth was Pie was actually also a little concerned but he didn't want his dad to catch on.

"What about diseases? He's always dating a different guy these days. I see it in these photos."

"Trust me, Dad, he's pretty sensible. You know Arm. We had dinner just two nights ago. He's fine. He's not dating all these guys, just paper talk. I've always got my eye on him. Don't worry, and don't get Mum worried!"

They then moved on to more standard small talk, before Sapong said he needed to get back. There then followed a familiar conversation where Pie tried to convince his old man to retire. On this occasion, Pie actually felt he had made some progress as Sapong replied, "One day, Pie, one day." The closest he'd ever got to even considering stopping work!

TWENTY TWO

As the days rolled on Bob continued to find juggling his caseload an increasingly challenging and stressful exercise, and now Daeng had informed him of this possible case via his friend Sapong, which would mean more work, potentially. He felt he needed to really push on with the tuk-tuk case, especially as Daeng was now proving to be a useful ally, and perhaps soon to be his landlord and roommate. The least he could do was prove his skills by solving this case.

Bob was very wary of the drugs issue, with his prior history of briefly being involved in the smuggling game with his former friend Alf Hayes. He didn't want to get involved too deep and still had a paranoid fear of being found out for his actions the previous year. If this was proved to be a drug dealing game he would immediately contact Khun Pun at the Royal Thai Police. No mucking around. He decided he would try and make direct contact with the 'drug lord' and then continue for a day or so to do his step by step stakeout. He still hadn't confirmed where the young man was going with the goods. He had assumed the young man took the ya ice that the old woman had given him to a string of street dealers, but he had to confirm this. *No assumptions, Lowe. Always get proof*, he had scrawled in his list of rules.

He sat back in place outside the old woman's house and sure enough, like clockwork she walked down the soi with the bags and table as before. Before walking towards her he made some more notes:

Are these the same bags that she loaded into the tuk-tuk at 5:30am?

Why has she now got the empties? Where is the man she gave them to?

He got up and strolled towards the woman, and managed to battle through a conversation in his finest Thai.

"Hello! How are you?" he asked confidently.

"Good."

"My name is Khun Bob, my friend tells me you are the best cook in town."

"Thank you very much! Maybe I am!"

Bob was getting nervous, she wasn't denying a thing! Utterly remarkable!

He looked from side to side, to make it absolutely clear that he didn't want to be overheard and that this was classified.

In whispered tones he said to her, "I want be customer. How?"

"Too late! Sold out for today! I don't sell here!"

"Of course, of course. Too dangerous!" Lowe

nodded wisely.

The woman looked slightly blank but smiled politely, and then, as so many Thai conversations went for Bob, he started to lose track of what she was saying. She pointed in the direction she came from and he was sure she mentioned the BTS.

Bob did lots of nodding and managed to end the conversation with a cheerful, "See you next time."

The woman smiled, and chuckled. She was clearly bemused by this chap.

Bob raced round the corner to Daeng's house and sat on one of the wooden stalls outside. Daeng had gone off to work already but he was sure he would have no objections to him sitting there, this was, after all, about to become his home. Perhaps.

He quickly wrote up the incident. He had already learnt that unless he wrote things up immediately then his memory would begin to fade.

Woman seemed to confirm her drug production – no denial.

She didn't seem happy at me asking to buy from her house.

Top work from The Lowe, got her right out of her comfort zone.

Her main distributors must operate from around the Skytrain stations – no doubt it's always busy there and thus easy to blend in.

Slick operator, one would never guess she was a drug baron. Remarkable situation.

Bob sat and pondered. What to do next? He still hadn't found out exactly what was going on with the tuk-tuk and now he was getting himself deep into another, albeit connected case. He vowed to take the next step in his tuk-tuk following the next morning. Though it was now obvious to him, she needed a vehicle to transport her drugs to her distributors at the BTS. She couldn't use her own vehicle as it would link back to her, so she used Daeng's so that if there was any issue with the police, Daeng would be the one to face the music. At some point he would have to break this news to Daeng. Also he had to consider the confusing matter of her stashing the drugs in that vehicle outside her house. The wise old girl, she'd probably claim to the police that it had been dumped there if anyone suspected anything.

Bob strolled back down the soi towards the BTS, he was feeling quite excited about the prospect of becoming Daeng's lodger and vowed to start packing his bags as soon as he got back to Susie's apartment. When he arrived at the Irish pub he couldn't resist popping in for a pint of Guinness, sure it wasn't a perfect pint of Guinness but as he told the waitress, "When in Ireland, my dear!" This led to a confused conversation in which she thought he was Irish. One pint quickly became three and Bob knew he was getting close to the point of no return. Generally speaking, Bob could drink two to three pints socially, but once Bob Lowe hit four pints, that was it. He would end up doing a marathon drinking session. As a clear sign of 'New Lowe' he paid up and continued his walk to the Skytrain station. Quickly stopping by his favourite pork noodles stall. He took a photo of his bowl of noodles and sent it to Pat.

"Still the best."

"Am I? Oh thanks Bob. 555."

Pat then sent Bob an almost identical photo as she

too was sitting down for a quick meal.

"We same same, Bob."

This sent tingles down Bob's spine. He slurped his noodles and muttered repeatedly, "Pat Lowe. Patty Lowe. Pat and The Lowe. Hmmmm."

He texted Pat and asked her to call Daeng about the room. Within minutes she had texted back and said that Daeng was totally laid back, Bob could turn up whenever he was ready as long as he had three thousand baht for his first month's rent in advance.

"Remarkable arrangement."

On his return to Susie's apartment, Bob quietly packed his few suitcases and decided to leave her a note, to avoid another confrontation.

Dear Susie,

Many thanks for allowing me to sleep on your sofa. Much appreciated, but my dear old friend Khun Daeng has a spare room which I will move into. It will help me solve the case too. Wonderful chap, Daeng. Salt of the earth. Old school. Proper Thai. Marvellous. What a character.
I think this will be best for all concerned. Enjoy the wine!

Yours etc.
Bob Lowe (PI)

Bob attached the note to a bottle of wine – the cheapest bottle he could find in Tesco Lotus, from their imported stock. He struggled out with his three large suitcases and an old sports bag flung over his shoulder and battled his way into the lift and onto the soi to get a taxi.

By eight o'clock that evening Bob was sitting outside the house with Daeng and Nat enjoying a beer and some khaw man gai. "This is the life!" Bob exclaimed. "This, Daeng. Is. The. Life." Daeng apparently agreed.

TWENTY THREE

Avi sat back with his ice-cold bottle of San Miguel Light and was quickly lost, deep in thought. He had exchanged his usual banter with Mint, who was on good form, as always. It amazed him how Mint always seemed to be so happy and positive, yet he himself was always lurching from one apparent crisis to another and was forever at a crossroads in his life. Here he was at sixty, retired and sitting in a bar in Bangkok, once again pondering the metaphorical junction he was at. The only issue tended to be that Avi wasn't clear what the signs said and therefore could barely begin to consider which way he was meant to turn.

By most accounts, Avi was one of life's lucky ones. Things had always fallen into place for him. He'd always had steady employment and the financial security that enabled him to have choices in life, and yet he often felt miserable. He sat alone on this busy Bangkok soi thinking about all of life's 'what ifs' as he was accustomed to doing. He had been born into relative privilege in Israel. His father was one of the most important figures in the Israeli Defence Force, a man who counted Ariel Sharon as one of his friends. Avi had begun to rebel against his father as soon as he could remember. Sol Shielmann not only had a passion for his country but he doubled that with a passion for his country's military might. Avi found this hard to accept. Like every Israeli, Avi had to spend some time in the army, and in the late 1970s and early 1980s this meant being involved in real and dangerous combat. On one particular mission, three of Avi's closest friends were killed in an instant from a homemade yet powerful explosive device. Avi miraculously survived, walking away totally unharmed, but he was mentally scarred for life by what he had seen. Sol had tried to use this tragedy as a way to open Avi's eyes to his point of view. Avi was even more appalled by his father's attitude. However, his father did have enough love and compassion for his son to be able to pull some strings and have him released from his military duties and then provided him with the funds for world travel, which was when Avi began to immerse himself in the disco scene. When he returned to Israel he did so with a real feeling of positivity about a new beginning, but he quickly grew tired. Tired of being an Israeli with his particular liberal views – it was exhausting. He was forever arguing with people, especially those of his father's generation about what the path to peace might be. For Avi it meant accepting some wrong-doing, concessions, discussion, negotiations, and compromise. For many older Israelis this was an absurd notion. They would patronise the youngsters like Avi who they felt didn't grasp the reality of the 'unique' situation. This was only half of the story though, when he travelled or met foreigners he often found himself entrenched in a different argument, defending his country. So many people outside Israel just had no idea that there were many people like Avi who felt little affinity with the actions of his country's government. They inevitably could fall back on an argument of 'well you would say that' or 'you're emotionally involved so...' It was infuriating, and ultimately these endless arguments just broke his spirit. In his mid-thirties he had turned his back on Israel. It was the right move, he had no regrets, and yet he was still wracked by guilt. Being Swedish was just so much easier. It was fascinating for him to see the different reaction he got when meeting new people as a Swede. People liked Swedes and the little they knew about Swedish culture was always positive. Bjorn Borg, Abba, Ikea, a perceived relaxed attitude to sex. How could anyone not like Sweden?

Yes, Avi was lucky, surely. He had always had a good job, he was easily able to move to Sweden and establish himself. He then met Ingrid, who was to become the love of his life. In fact on meeting Ingrid he suddenly became aware that she was the second love of his life. He realised then that he had been in love with Mo Razzaq. Not in a sexual way, Avi wasn't gay, but in a deeper more meaningful way. He became aware that for years he had been mourning the loss of Mo from his life.

Meeting Ingrid was a turning point in Avi's life and he started to become a much more positive person. She worked in his office. She would typically be unfairly described as 'plain', 'not unattractive' or the equally bland 'pleasant'. Avi fell in love. They would chat for hours and quickly became the closest of friends. Eventually, Avi plucked up the courage to tell Ingrid how he felt. He broke down in tears, they embraced. She felt the same way and confessed to Avi that she had never properly dated anyone. Here she was at the age of thirty, embarking on a new life. For four months Avi was skipping around town. Yes, he was lucky and now the one thing that had eluded him had fallen into place; he was in love and in a loving relationship. It all came crashing down though. Just after their four-month anniversary (yes they had celebrated it!), Ingrid was diagnosed with breast cancer. Within six months of that diagnosis she was taken from Avi. He was crushed. That was it for him. Love just wasn't worth the pain and misery. Eventually he settled into a comfortable yet monotonous existence. The few who knew him well, knew that something was missing from his life.

Thus it could be said that the two clear aspects of Avi's personality were guilt and missing loves. He still felt a deep guilt about how he had abandoned his country of birth, but also how he had fallen out with and essentially abandoned Mo Razzaq. At sixty he was sure it was too late to fix any of this, but he did wonder if he could still find a version of happiness.

Avi was snapped out of his daydream by the vision of Bob Lowe stumbling his way into Mints. For a moment he considered the possibility that Bob was very, very drunk, but he soon learnt that this was a sober stumbling, unique to Bob Lowe.

"Avi, my dear old thing, how's things?"

"You know, Bob, plodding along."

"Aren't we all? So you're becoming a Mints regular then."

"Oh yes, it's my favourite bar even if I've always thought Mints was an odd name for such a place."

"Don't get The Lowe started on that damn missing apostrophe!"

At that Mint wandered over to take Bob's order.

"Where's that apostrophe, Mint?! Add it! Mint's. Mint's Bar. Mint's Place." Bob had been through this many times.

"No, Bob! Mints. I eat Mints always." Mint laughed, she knew it annoyed Bob.

"But it's a bar! Not a sweet shop! I'll have the same as Avi, but no mints, Mint!"

Bob roared with laughter, he was doing this partly for Avi's benefit.

"So, Bob, any progress on my case?" Avi enquired.

"The wheels are very much turning, the wheels are turning."

"You've found Mohammed?"

"Well strictly speaking, at the moment I've found millions of Mohammeds. Just leave this to The Lowe." With that Bob unfurled an A4 poster that Pat had mocked up for him.

'Disco is back! Avi Shielmann, former World Disco sensation, in Mints bar!'

He showed it to Avi "We'll have you back dancing in no time."Avi looked at Bob in shock, and his eyes began to moisten. Bob added "A Bob Lowe promotion. Avi Shielmann; the return." Both men laughed as they enthusiastically slugged on their beers.

They sat together in silence, watching an expat guy of about thirty begin to flirt with one of the waitresses. Bob gave Avi a knowing look. "We all know where this is ending."

"What's the appeal? What's it all about?" mused

Avi.

"Er. Sex I believe, old boy. Some speak rather highly…" Bob began prattling as he wiped the sweat from his brow.

"But this whole situation, the girls, the money." Avi waved his arm around. "And he's a young chap. He doesn't need to pay for it."

"Well, if my many years in Bangkok have taught me anything, Avi, my friend, it's that it's so much more complicated than that. Some of them end up married."

"Have you ever thought about marrying a girl from a bar, Bob?" Avi began to think about his own near-marriage and inevitably his words took on a melancholic tone.

"I won't lie. I've known a few bar girls in my time. But, you know what, Avi. Can I be honest? I don't think I've got the guts."

Avi gave a puzzled look before Bob continued to explain.

"I'm embarrassed to admit it, but ultimately I've worried about what people will think. Bob Lowe shacked up with a Thai woman years younger than him. They'd be cynical. But I feel awful saying this out loud."

Across the bar the guy they had been watching was now flirting with a different girl. Avi pondered the futility of it all and the attitude of the men. Women were very much objects to be purchased in the eyes of these guys. He let Bob's words hang in the air.

"No need to be ashamed, Bob. You're not one of the bad guys. You just need to meet the right one. I did once."

Bob detected the sadness in Avi's voice and

decided not to pry.

"Ah, the one, yes indeed. But what if the one for me doesn't think I am the one for her. Story of my life. It'd make a good book you know, the failings in love of Bob Lowe. 'The diary of Bob Lowe; Loser in love', it'd be too tragic to believe!"

"Two more?" Mint enquired as she approached the table.

"Two more," they replied in unison.

TWENTY FOUR

Bob had decided that it would soon be time to report the drug smuggling to the police as he was certainly not keen to get involved in a major drug issue. Although, of course, he wondered if, with the nature of his new job, this was a reality he simply couldn't avoid. Perhaps Bob Lowe could be the man to sort out Thailand's drug problem. Bob of course would push for a much more liberal attitude to drug use. Back in the day, Bob had dabbled in any drug he could get his hands on, and as he told anyone who would listen, "never did me any harm!" With Bob easily able to pass for a man fifteen years older and with the memory of a man forty years older, many would beg to differ.

Now that he was living in Daeng's house he had something of a dilemma. He could of course simply wait for the tuk-tuk thief, but it was clear he was a young man and if apprehended by Bob he could simply run off. Bob needed to know exactly what was going on so then he could take a slick dossier to

Khun Pun, his police buddy.

Bob was not finding it easy sleeping at Daeng's as he had no A/C in his spare room. Bob had been spoilt by his stay at Susie's with the room extra-cold at night. The fan splattered around and Bob woke drenched in sweat, even though it hadn't yet reached the hottest time of the year. He had to ensure he left the house well before the Tuk-tuk thief so that he could be positioned on the street corner, the latest one he had reached, in plenty of time. He left the house at 4:30 am and walked the long route so he could pop into 7-Eleven for a cappuccino on the way.

He walked down the soi and marvelled at the silence. He did love early mornings even if he wasn't always able to wake up in time to appreciate it. Once he had reached Silom Road there was a little bit more life and a few drunk tourists staggering about looking for somewhere to get some food.

"Ah, the old false hunger, such naivety," Bob muttered to himself. He had learnt at an early age that money spent on food while drunk was simply money wasted. What he called a 'false hunger', it was the booze tricking you. Bob simply drank his way through it, and if he was out of cash he would drink pints of water to defeat the hunger. That was another chapter in his unfinished masterpiece 'Bob Lowe's thrifty Bangkok living.'

He walked back around the block to reach the side soi and the latest corner he had reached. After his discussion with the old woman he was sure he would just need to watch the tuk-tuk back to Silom Road, she had basically told him that her team of drug dealers operated from a spot close to the Skytrain station.

He sat down by a small shrub growing through the tarmac. A sleeping soi dog lifted his head at the intrusion, then went back to sleep as if he was thinking 'oh it's just Bob Lowe'. Bob nodded at the dog, to thank him for not giving him any bother. Another of Bob's key Bangkok rules, "Respect the soi dog and the soi dog will respect you." He had never been attacked by a dog and therefore was certain his policy was obviously correct.

Bob settled himself near the corner of Silom Road, with a view down the soi to the corner that he had reached with his step by step stakeout. After ten or fifteen minutes sitting and slurping his coffee he saw the tuk-tuk pull out of the soi. "Gotcha," Bob whispered and took a photo with his cheap smartphone. The photo was basically a light in the distance, such was the low resolution of his camera phone.

As he expected the tuk-tuk drove past him, turned onto the Silom Road and stopped just by the BTS entrance!

The young chap began to set up a table and took out the bags of what Bob was sure must contain bags of little red yaba pills.

Remarkable. The chap seems to be setting up a drug stall by the BTS. Police involved? Bob wrote in his notes.

He sat and watched as the young man unloaded his wares and appeared to be laying them out on display. Bob was too far away to see exactly but he was staggered by what was going on. Before he got up, he got another shock. The old woman began to walk her way down the soi.

She's going to sell the drugs herself! He furiously scribbled in his notes, and after another fifteen minutes the young man had set up the drug shop and was racing away with the tuk-tuk. *Returned to Daeng. Slick drug dealers for sure.*

He decided he would subtly stroll past the stall and see what was going on and how she was disguising her illicit wares. As he reached the woman she instantly recognised him and said to him in Thai, "Now you can buy some."

He looked down stunned, and saw on the table an array of delicious fried pork items, chicken wings and other delicacies. He regained his composure. "Moo grob khrap." He ordered some of his favourite crispy pork. He walked away eating it, it was indeed delicious, crispy yet chewy. Amazing.

He sat down back on the steps by his favourite 7-Eleven, and began to feel quite nervous and panicked.

They are clearly on to me, and to protect their multi-million-dollar business they have set up a pork stall.

Correction, they sell drugs inside the bags of pork! Of course! Simplicity personified.

Confirm over next few days then hand dossier to Pun.

"Breakfast at the Lumpini," Bob informed the soi as he got up and walked down to the five-star hotel. The Lumpini Park Hotel was a Bangkok institution of faded grandeur, and for Bob it was glorious. None of the flashy opulence of these new places. "Proper old-world style and classy service." Bob would tell anyone. He shouldn't really be splashing his cash on expensive breakfasts, but he knew he would eat enough to need no further meals that day; just the odd snack perhaps.

"Table for The Lowe, just the one. One Lowe!"

The staff at the Lumpini were impeccably trained and even some classic 'Lowespeak' couldn't knock them off their stride.

"Certainly, sir. What room number?"

"Oh, I'm not staying here, just popped in to ease my appetence, so to speak. Lowe lives nearby, lovely old house down Soi Pipat."

He was led to a table and the waitress asked for his drink order.

"Coffee, please. Just to check, I can have unlimited coffees, yes?"

"Yes, sir. No problem."

"And it's still all you can eat?"

"Yes, sir."

"As many visits to the buffet as I require?"

The waitress confirmed before Bob added, "The Lowe's been caught out before. Phnom Penh, a decade or so back. Frightful business, and quite a bill I might tell you."

Lowe always began what he tended to refer to as an LBB (Lumpini Breakfast Buffet) with some steamed Chinese dumplings. Where most people would take two or three, Lowe covered his plate. He noticed a curious glance from a middle-aged tourist (Korean, Bob guessed). As Bob walked back to his table he bellowed, "Gotta love the dumplings at an LBB," before clumsily thumping the plate down on his table and spilling his dipping sauce.

TWENTY FIVE

Bob's recent exchange with the lady selling fried pork had confused him slightly. He pondered whether he was taking the wrong approach to be now focusing on her rather than the tuk-tuk thief himself.

"It's a question of morality, Nong Pat. She's selling drugs, right there on the soi! Disguising herself as a pork seller, it's shocking," he explained to Pat when he went to meet her for lunch next to his old language school, where Pat still worked.

"Hold it, you can't be sure of this. Isn't it possible she's just selling pork on the soi?" Pat was trying to explain to Bob that sometimes the simple explanation was the correct one.

"Oh, I am well aware of that possibility, Pat, but when one is an experienced private investigator one has to be capable of balancing all the possibilities. I know enough about drugs in this city to know the simple explanation is rarely correct!"

"You know drugs?!" Pat was aware that Bob was a bit of a character and she had smoked a few joints herself, but Bob saw her as very innocent.

"Well I mean, I've been here many years, my dear Pat, I mean The Lowe in his youth, well I'm a changed man, of course, not myself, but you know what I mean. Well anyway, where was I?"

Pat couldn't help but start giggling. She was enjoying her new developing friendship with Bob. She had always got on very well with him, and unknown to Bob there was a time when she had hoped he would ask her on a date, but he never did. She had noticed that after a few months working there he displayed all the signs of someone who had got deep into the drinking and womanising scene. She had heard the conversations that the teachers in the staff room had and it saddened her. She still couldn't help but like Bob though, he was such a hopeless character and so quirky that it made her laugh.

One of those conversations in the staff room particularly stuck in her memory because a young female American teacher had tried to officially complain about the men and the way they spoke. On this occasion an argument broke out about where the best prostitutes in town were to be found and then, what they thought was a more nuanced debate about where the best *value* was to be found. It was of course shocking but Pat had got used to overhearing this sort of thing. Bob didn't say much but she heard his voice mutter a few times, "Nana, always Nana." One rather odious chap piped in, "Nana? Nana!? Third rate hookers, *at best*. You've got to be more open-minded and creative here."

That particular chap, Tony, was especially objectionable in Pat's eyes. He had moved in with and subsequently married a bar girl very early in his time in Bangkok and was then pontificating about 'Thai women' and how they were. It outraged Pat as he had no idea what he was talking about, just stereotyping and judging based on his limited experience. Not only was his experience limited only to bar girls, but even there his experience was minimal having so quickly settled with one. When he had got married he had paid a huge amount as a dowry, sinsod in Thai, that had shocked most in the know, but he'd say, "That's how it goes with Thai women, mate, all about the cash. Everyone pays it, most probably pay more."

Pat was daydreaming and Bob was irritated. "Pat! Are you listening?"

"Sorry, Bob, mind thinking, na. What happened to Tony, where is he now?"

"Tony? The chap from school? Goodness didn't you hear?"

"No, no. What?"

Bob explained that the woman he had married had drained him of all his money. She had opened a business, and it was obvious to all except Tony that he had given her much more money than she needed. She barely worked there anyway. He had paid thousands to her family, and then finally their apartment in Asok had been broken into, all his valuables stolen. The thief had a key. It was quickly apparent that Tony's wife had another long-term boyfriend who she had known since she was seventeen. It took a long time for the penny to drop but eventually Tony realised that their marriage was basically a sham, or even a scam, and they had broken up. Tony had sold his apartment giving more than half the money to his wife who was living back in her hometown with their only child. She was denying

Tony access to the kid, spreading rumours that he was a bad father and a cheating husband. A real mess. Tony had put on about twenty-five kilos in weight and was drinking heavily, lost his job, and had to take a gig earning significantly lower wages at a mediocre language school, back where he had started.

"The poor chap's in a real state." Bob felt genuinely empathetic towards his old colleague.

Pat was clearly insincere. "Oh, that so sad." Inside she was feeling a touch of schadenfreude, she had never liked Tony. He was rude, arrogant and very ignorant. She felt he had got what he deserved.

"Anyway, back to the pork drugs. I have contacts with the police, I just need to confirm this and then report it. The next two days I will monitor. Are you free for lunch in two days? I'd like your view before I go to the police."

Pat was impressed how professional Bob seemed to be, but she was sure the truth was much simpler. Surely this woman wasn't really dealing drugs, but Bob did seem to have a lot of evidence. Naïve as Bob thought she was, Pat had simply never heard of an old woman living in a nice quiet street in Silom, while dealing in drugs.

Pat had to rush back to work, so Bob thought he'd pop to a nearby Starbucks to see what all the fuss was about. He knew he was going to find it expensive but he couldn't hold back when the barista told him the price.

"For a *small* cappuccino? Good Lord! Better get a new bank loan!"

The server ignored him.

Bob had to admit the coffee was nice and that it was very pleasant sitting in a cold air con environment with plenty of magazines and papers to read. He was determined to get his money's worth.

He thought through his discussion with Pat. Fancy Pat throwing me an Occam's razor, he pondered. "I invented Occam's razor, should be called Lowe's razor," he muttered under his breath. He had been careful not to patronise her, and he was determined not to reveal his intimate relationship with the Bangkok drug scene, but Pat was terribly naïve in Bob's eyes. It was pretty certain that the suspicious behaviour of the tuk-tuk thief and his accomplice was a sign of something illegal. He would accept drugs was not a certainty, but something dodgy most definitely was.

A farang guy approached him. Bob looked up, thinking the worst. There was nothing more annoying than some dodgy farang who wanted to chat with random people in a café. Bob tried to focus on his reading of the Bangkok Post and ignore the guy.

"Interesting article that, don't you think?"

Bob looked up from what he was reading – an article about a Spanish man who was trying to start an environmental movement in Chiang Mai.

"Yes, I suppose," Bob muttered, disinterested.

"Wonderfully well written, wouldn't you say?" the chap persisted.

"Well, it's certainly pretty solid." Bob tried to ignore the guy.

"I'm only pulling your leg. I'm John Albertson, I wrote it!"

"Good Lord! John Albertson! I've been reading your articles for years. Wonderfully insightful." Bob was suddenly interested.

"Always nice to meet a fan! Sorry, I didn't catch

your name?" John spoke with a particular accent and Bob instantly clocked him as a classic upper middle class Brit in Thailand.

"Bob Lowe, you may have heard of me, I'm..." Bob looked round and then spoke in hushed tones, "one of the top private investigators in the city."

"Fascinating! Utterly fascinating. I mean genuinely utterly fascinating!"

Bob sensed a kindred spirit. They chatted for a while and Bob felt guilty for his initially dismissing John as a weird random farang. They exchanged business cards, and Bob not so subtly suggested that John might want to run a feature on his PI business. Anonymous, no names of course.

TWENTY SIX

Marjorie was very happy with her developing friendship with Linda Taylor. She was acutely aware that she needed an ally if she was to confirm that Gladys was indeed stealing from the women's society funds. The system the BWBLS ran was simple, perhaps too simple Marjorie had mused to Linda. Each week the women would pay fifteen hundred baht into the pot, literally. They had an ornate brass pot that would sit on the table and when the women arrived for their weekly bridge session they would put their cash in. This would cover the costs for tea, coffee and snacks at the weekly venue. Lunch, if they had lunch, would be paid for. In the old days they would always have a lavish lunch, hence the name of the society. But over the years more and more women were becoming health conscious and finding a weekly buffet lunch wasn't an especially good idea. The money that was left in the kitty would go towards some other events, but more importantly it would form the basis of their charitable giving. They would make a string of donations at least twice yearly to charities that some of the members would put forwards to the BWBLSCC – the Bangkok Women's Bridge and Lunch Society Charitable Committee. Usually simply referred to as the 'CC'.

"How do you think she is doing this?" Linda asked Marjorie on a recent coffee outing.

"I can't be sure, Linda, but from our last meeting, you'll remember she arrived late? Rather than put money into the kitty she simply takes a few notes out. I was watching carefully and I am sure this is what she did."

"Of course! She *is* always late. But more importantly why is she doing this?" Linda was excited by the drama and scandal but she couldn't get her head round it.

"I can only imagine it's…" Marjorie paused, putting her hand to her forehead, "dementia. Oh, it's too awful."

"Maybe she just needs the cash," Linda said.

Trust Linda to think it was all about the grubby business of cash, thought Marjorie before she gave it some consideration.

"Surely not? Gladys and Chanatip are very wealthy." Marjorie dismissed the suggestion.

"Well, all this travelling by BTS, at her age. What if it is actually all about necessity rather than some kind of environmental crusade?" Linda thought this was a genuinely plausible idea.

"I just don't know, Linda dear. Oh, poor Gladys."

The two women discussed a plan and agreed that on no account should they call the police. They didn't want to humiliate Gladys, they just wanted to help her. Marjorie neglected to tell Linda that she had informed her dear friend John Albertson, Bangkok Post feature writer. She had told John that she would not allow him to write a story without her say so and he would never be able reveal his source. John, of course, agreed. He had known Marjorie for years.

By a remarkable coincidence both John and her driver Sapong had mentioned this Bob Lowe chap. A farang working as a PI in the city. It must be written in the stars she thought. Sapong and John Albertson hardly moved in the same circles. From the way John had described this Bob Lowe character, she thought he would be perfect as a low-key person to confirm the shocking and terrible truth.

She had arranged to meet Bob at a Starbucks outlet close to On Nut, very early one Sunday morning. She hadn't been down to that part of town for years and years and was amazed at how it had changed. Fashionable condos and lots of them, cute little cafés, and a few respectable looking shopping malls.

"Well I never, Sapong, just look at On Nut!"

"Yes, Khun Marjorie. Very beautiful."

Marjorie wasn't sure she'd go quite that far but it had certainly improved.

Bob Lowe couldn't quite believe what was happening. This business was more than just taking off, now he had the wife of the former British ambassador asking him to meet and discuss a 'rather delicate matter' as she had put it over the phone.

He looked through his wardrobe and really didn't know what to wear. His normal attire certainly wasn't appropriate for an ambassadorial meeting. Then he remembered, on his most recent trip to the UK he had found some wonderful gems in the charity shops he loved perusing. He took his linen suit and Panama hat out of the wardrobe and was rather pleased with himself. He had longed for the right occasion to wear these and give himself the confidence to start to dress this way more regularly. The empire was dead but Bob still believed the fineries of colonial Britain could live on.

He arrived early and settled himself down with a caramel macchiato. "Marvellous," he said rather too loudly as he took his first sip, alerting curious glances from the smattering of people who were enjoying an early morning coffee or snack.

It was plainly obvious to him when Marjorie arrived, she really was not your typical On Nut foreigner. Bob had very much categorised On Nut as a zone for 'mid-ranking' expats. Not the so-called 'Nana Dwellers' who spent all their time in Bangkok's seedy bars, but close enough to be able to have regular nights out there. On Nut was pleasant, with a bit of an edge compared to the city's more fashionable areas.

"Mr Bob Lowe, I presume?"

Bob was instantly impressed with the manner in which Marjorie spoke.

"Marjorie Dubshott. Charmed to meet you." Bob instantly morphed into 'Lowe – sophisticated British gent'.

Marjorie explained the situation, casually dropping the name of Gladys Suprawongse and then telling Bob she really shouldn't have told him the name, since Gladys was such a well-known figure in Thailand.

"Discretion personified. Client confidentiality. Whatever you say to Bob Lowe, stays between us."

Bob found it to be a terribly sad case, which he scrawled in his notes. Dear Gladys had clearly lost her marbles. He actually wrote *lost her marbles* then crossed it out for *Alzheimer's?* as he felt even his notes should be following politically correct policies. He thought he should add that to Bob's charter. It could be very important. What if they were ever needed in court?

Marjorie wanted Bob to witness what was going on and if possible to keep the police out of the matter.

"Absolutely! Bob Lowe only involves the police when clients agree," he stated proudly. Then he began to wonder what he would do if a client confessed to a murder or he witnessed a murder. He would then have to break his own confidentiality rules.

"Except in case of murder," he hastily added.

"What?" Marjorie was somewhat taken aback.

"I mean, you know, a big murder case. Then I always involve the police. I mean, I have to, oh sorry. Moving on, you were saying. Gladys… whoops, I mean the lady in question."

At that moment Marjorie realised that John's description of Bob was spot on and he was indeed the perfect person for her to involve in this investigation.

After Marjorie had departed, Bob took the opportunity to have a wander around the Tesco Lotus at the Skytrain station. He always felt something of an affinity with the area around On Nut; it was the first place he had ever lived in Bangkok, which of course in that era was the final station on the line. He fondly remembered how the lights on the train would flash when they reached the station to inform people it was the last stop, something that had often proved very useful for a daydreaming Lowe. He decided to have a stroll around the locality to visit his old apartment. He quickly regretted the decision, despite it being early morning the LST (Lowe Sweat Time) seemed to be higher than usual and with the new malls and fancy condominiums he quickly got confused by which soi it was he had actually lived on. He decided it would be prudent to abandon the idea and head back to his new home in Silom. He had settled in well to Daeng's house and felt like he was really living the Thai life. Daeng made him coffee every morning and he enjoyed chewing the fat with Daeng and Nat, even if he could add little to the conversation. He would also regularly sit out in the evening with Daeng (and sometimes Nat) with a bottle of whisky or sang som or just a couple of beers. There were many farang around Silom but Bob was almost certain he was the only one living on this tiny sub soi. With that he quickly became something of a local novelty.

Later that evening he sat back with a cold beer – Daeng had provided a big bag of ice – and talked over his various cases with Daeng. He had made it clear he could not possibly discuss the tuk-tuk case, as Daeng was personally involved. He did of course hint that it was becoming very complicated.

"So, Daeng. Pim like German man. But easy live with British man. He bad man." Bob's Thai was good enough for the basics. Daeng said little and nodded a lot. Occasionally he asked Bob a few questions. From what Bob could ascertain, Daeng felt that Pim should follow her heart. His logic was simple. "German man better than British man." Bob pretended to be very offended and they laughed and laughed.

"Anyway, Khun Daeng, off to Bedfordshire for

me. Another early start sorting out your tuk-tuk mess." Daeng had rather lost interest. He was getting regular one hundred-baht notes left by the thief and he was content, but Bob was enjoying himself and was curious to know what was going on.

"Bed-for-shy." Daeng was slowly picking up Bob's quirks.

The following morning Bob spent quite a while observing the 'pork 'n' drugs lady' (as he was now calling her) and he was perplexed. She was either slicker than he imagined or she was genuinely only selling fried pork. He wondered if he could possibly be wrong.

He texted Pat, *Not impossible we were right about the simple answer being correct. Still no hard evidence of drugs.*

Pat replied simply, *WE?!*

Well as a PI I have to be more careful with my thoughts, Nong Pat. Occam's razor. Yes. Agreed. Maybe.

Sometimes when Bob's messages were confusing, Pat just ignored them. This was such a time.

Bob had learnt about Occam's razor from a TV quiz show and he rather liked the theory that when presented with numerous possibilities the simple one is usually correct. It would become his core business model. Though of course he couldn't tell customers that. They wouldn't need him if they knew. He laughed to himself and went back home to Daeng's for a nap.

TWENTY SEVEN

After being shown the poster of the Avi Shielmann Disco Revival, Avi began to feel quite apprehensive. He hadn't danced properly for over thirty years. One could hardly count the occasional jive and shake that he'd had in Nana bars. True, he had always got a good reaction from both the waitresses and the punters but he'd wondered just how genuine that was. Far more likely they clapped and cheered at the novelty of a sixty-year-old guy just randomly getting up and strutting some disco moves. He chatted with Mint about this while enjoying one of his regular evening drinks.

"You dance very good, Mister Avi." She was trying to convince him that if he enjoyed the dancing then he should just go for it. Avi was aware that this was why Thailand was so good for him; Thai people tended to be able to break things down to the core root of the issue. Mint was spot on. She often joked that Avi thought too much. His long hours gazing out onto the soi with a beer in hand surely weren't that helpful. She was, of course, right. Mint's view was that sometimes things really were simple. Avi could look back and realise the hours and days, years even, that he had wasted worrying about the future or bemoaning the past. Really what he needed was to start living the present. He had begun to consider Mint as a friend, albeit not a friend in the most traditional sense. But over time they had developed quite a unique kinship. Mint had quickly ascertained that Avi wasn't interested in taking her home for a night or more, and as a result they both became more and more honest in their chats. They let their guard down as there was no pretence, no reason to lie.

"Why you never take a girl, Avi? You like boys?" Mint enquired matter-of-factly.

"No, no, Mint. Just not really looking for one night. Sex. That's easy. Sometimes it's boring." Avi was being totally frank.

"Yes. I think same."

Avi had noticed Mint was always in the bar and he had never seen her 'bar-fined' the term used for when a punter paid to take a woman away from the bar for an hour, or more.

"Same question for you, Mint. You never go with a customer, why?"

"Ha ha. Yes, that true." Mint then began to whisper, "Most customer ugly. I not interest."

Mint explained to Avi that her looks and friendly manner tended to result in a lot of lady drinks, and the commission for her was lucrative enough. While her salary may be low she made eighty baht for each drink that was 'bought' for her. Even on a bad night she'd still get about ten lady drinks. Sometimes it could go as high as thirty. On average, therefore, she was making about twelve hundred baht per night from the commissions. That was good enough for her. It just wasn't worth the hassle for a little bit extra to go off with a customer. She confided in Avi that she hadn't had sex for over three years, and she'd never been happier. Again, for Avi, Nana never ceased to amaze. Here he was chatting with a bar girl who was avoiding sex! He knew she was telling the truth; this wasn't a lie to try and interest a potential customer.

Her past had been full of too many bad experiences. For every easy fifteen hundred to two thousand baht she'd made there had been handfuls of drunk men who wanted to do obscene things with her, who didn't have enough money to pay, or who she'd be stuck with all night and have to wake them for her money in the morning. The list was endless. She'd vowed three years earlier that enough was enough. She had been bar-fined by a particularly arrogant British guy of about thirty-five. She was unsure about him but he said he'd pay two thousand five hundred and he didn't seem too drunk. When they got back to his condo he had three friends there and had just assumed that Mint would service them all.

"Okay, lads, who's going first?!" At that Mint was quick enough to dash for the door and find the lift still waiting on the same level. As she walked out of the building she told herself it was time to stop. She was sick and tired of the attitude of these men.

Avi was no longer shocked by the stories Mint told him. He'd heard it all on his visits to Bangkok, although at the same time Bangkok was always ready with another story at some time that beat all others.

Mint asked about Mo Razzaq.

"Who your friend Mo?" Mint had heard Avi talking with Bob.

"I did a terrible thing, Mint. So, so bad."

For the next twenty-five minutes, when Mint was able to break off from delivering beers and join Avi to chat, he proceeded to detail what had happened. For reasons he still didn't fully understand he had begun to feel a strong resentment of his friend. Was it simple jealousy that Mo was outdoing him on the disco circuit? Was it a feeling of anxiety that their disco journey was inevitably going to come to an end soon? He couldn't be sure and now looking back he couldn't remember what was going through his mind when he did what he did.

The result was humiliation and defeat for Mo when the world disco title was within his grasp. On the day before the final dance, Avi had seen Mo's favourite sequin outfit hanging in the dressing room. It was quiet, he was alone, and almost without thinking he picked it up and shoved it haphazardly down by the drains, covered in by a piece of plywood in the corner of the changing area. He didn't know what had come over him but once it was done, it was done. After a long search someone had found it, too dirty to wear, and it was clear to everyone that it could only have got there by a deliberate act. It sent shockwaves through the disco community that day. Avi's strange bitterness and anger didn't subside, and before the grand finale he took a screwdriver to Mo's disco shoes, loosening the heels. The result was spectacular. Less than a minute into the dance that was surely to lead Mo to disco glory, both heels flew off. Mo fell flat onto his back and was in agony. He couldn't continue. For a while people feared he may have done some serious damage having landed hard on his coccyx. Avi sat in the dressing room in tears. Only Mo realised why. When they were alone Mo looked at Avi. "Why?"

"Avi, why? You were my closest friend."

Avi walked out of the dressing room and they never spoke or saw each other again.

Mint's eyes were a bit moist.

"That so sad, Avi."

She found it hard to believe that someone as kind, and warm hearted as Avi could have done such a thing.

A tear rolled down Avi's left cheek and he quickly wiped it away.

"I still don't know why I did it, Mint. I still can't answer Mo's question. Why? Why?"

TWENTY EIGHT

Much as Bob was enjoying living in Daeng's old wooden house just off Soi Pipat he felt guilty about how he'd left things with Susie. He decided it was time to send a conciliatory message and ask her out for dinner to make up for his poor behaviour. He invited her to join him and Pat for a bite to eat and a few drinks. Susie had worked with Bob and Pat back in the day and she remembered Pat fondly. They had decided to go to a trendy new group of bars near to Central World.

Bob battled his way onto the Skytrain. In rush hour the whole system felt like it was at breaking point and he was uncomfortably squashed in. He tried to remain calm, closing his eyes and imagining he was somewhere else. Getting off the train was a whole other battle and Bob lurched into full-on angry farang mode as people tried to barge on before many had got off.

"For pity's sake! People getting off here! Hello! Long rot! Long rot!" When Bob was angry his Thai was impossible to understand, he just barked in a full British accent and people didn't even realise he was trying to speak in Thai. He made eye contact with a fellow farang, and they exchanged a little knowing glance and raise of the eyebrows. Bob grabbed the opportunity.

"The mind boggles. It really does. I love Thailand but honestly…" While the chap obviously agreed with the sentiment he didn't want to get embroiled in a cultural debate with Bob and he quickly dashed off. Bob marched to the far exit at the end of the platform only to find that it was an entrance only with just an up escalator.

"The giddy limit! This is the thin end of anyone's wedge," he roared as he stomped back to the stairs, sweat building up rapidly. By the time he reached Pat and Susie in the bar they were chuckling away happily with a bottle of wine while Bob was fully wound up.

"Never! I repeat, never, do I get the Skytrain at rush hour again. NEVER!"

"Oh, Bob… shut up!" Susie hollered.

"Yeh, Bob, don't ruin the vibe." Pat went into one of her trademark giggles.

Bob sat down, irritated but quiet. After ten minutes and a few long swigs of a Hoegarden rose he had calmed down.

"Nothing like a cold fruit juice to calm the old nerves. Back in the Zen Lowe mode now."

Susie and Pat laughed hilariously, Bob couldn't help but join them as he realised himself the utter lunacy of the word Zen being combined with Lowe.

He thanked Susie for her hospitality and explained that his irritation and impatience with her was probably out of shame of having to live on her sofa.

Both women had noticed that Bob was becoming more perceptive these days.

"Where I live now, well you wouldn't call it slick and stylish but it's real. Deliciously real. Daeng, well he's like the best friend I'd never met. Wonderful chap. Truly wonderful."

As Bob slurped on his third strawberry beer he had managed to totally forget the irritating Skytrain incident.

"Some of my mates call this a lady's beer, but by gosh it tastes good. Lowe is fully in touch with his feminine side." He took another hearty gulp.

"Er, lady's beer? That's a bit sexist." Susie had a furious look on her face, that caused all her wrinkles to show.

"Well come on, strawberry juice in beer? It's hardly macho."

Pat then joined in. "Oh, Bob! You *are* sexist!"

"Good Lord, ladies, I'm not saying women can't drink beer. Goodness me they can booze as well as the next guy, I've known a few in my time…"

With that Pat and Susie burst into laughter again.

"Oh for fuck's sake! You two characters."

Bob downed his pint and thumped the empty glass down on the table and roared, "What woman does that?"

Bob wasn't sure how he felt about this Susie and Pat double act. He began to wonder if Susie could put in a good word for him. Tell Pat just how he felt. That was just it though. He wasn't quite sure how he felt about her.

"Bob! Stop daydreaming." Susie gave a trademark toothy grin as she spoke.

"Sorry, miles away. Busy week for me."

"Do you ever hear from Alf Hayes anymore?" This was the first time either of them had mentioned his name since the infamous evening when he'd humiliated the pair of them. Susie didn't even know that Bob had been doubly humiliated by being scammed on the drug deal he had foolishly got involved with.

"Not a word since. Well you know. That night." Susie gave a partly sad, partly patronising smile.

"Better off without him. You wouldn't believe the circles I move in now! Ambassadors and their ilk." Bob began to embellish the facts somewhat.

"I've also had a very interesting meeting with John Albertson, yes, he of Bangkok Post fame."

Bob explained that he couldn't go into details, but, 'who knows where that could lead?' "I suspect he has a case for The Lowe. No doubt that's why he approached me. Word's getting about I can tell you. Taking off."

"So what about you, Susie? I heard you split from Tong. So sorry." Pat changed the subject. "How are you coping, na?"

"Thanks for asking, Pat, you're so sweet." Susie glanced at Bob as she said this.

"It's not been easy. Tong is back in Nong Khai, I think. Probably with some boyfriend."

"Oh! I see." Pat wasn't really surprised by this. Even on their wedding day in that nice Bangkok hotel, Pat had never quite felt Tong was really that into Susie.

"Men, eh?"

The two women clinked their glasses together. "Bloody men. Sick of them."

"Er... hello! I am sitting right here."

"Oh, come on, you're not a man!" Pat found this hilarious.

"Now who's the sexist one? I mean if I made a comment like that. The double standards, it really does go beyond..."

"Shut up!" Again the two women spoke in unison and laughed hilariously.

Bob found it hard enough to navigate his way through equality issues and the like. These sort of exchanges often confused him. What were the bloody rules? They can joke? When can I? Bob wasn't sexist, he considered himself a modern man and believed in equality for all, but he kept getting himself into murky waters by his use of language. It was infuriating.

He managed to change the subject, which was one skill he had learnt. *Quit when you're down, Lowe!*

He updated Pat on his cases. She interrupted him with the odd insightful comment to keep him on the right track, and to try and keep his more absurd suggestions from the forefront of his brain.

Susie was seriously impressed and rather amazed. To her complete shock, Bob was actually making a success of his PI business, it seemed. He had clients, leads, and was making contacts with some impressive people. She felt strangely proud of how he was doing.

TWENTY NINE

Bob had spent many hours and days agonising over a plan with regards the tuk-tuk/drugs/pork case. The result being that he didn't succeed in formulating much of a plan. However, he did manage to get a bit of clarity, largely helped by a simple text message from Pat, *Remember the case is about the tuk-tuk*

"Classic Pat," he mused as he sat in Starbucks the next morning, enjoying a cappuccino. Bob had noticed that slowly he had begun to embrace the pricier café as he could spend hours sitting and reading newspapers, and no one cared. He also felt flush with cash as the money was relatively pouring in. The following day he would start the day on the tuk-tuk case and then head to the Lumpini Park Hotel for his first attempt to assess the theft case that he had been hired by Marjorie Dubshott to solve. Bob had spent some time on the internet researching about the Dubshotts and the Suprawongses and was framing some ideas in his mind.

"Oh, John!" Bob noticed John Albertson walk into the café, and so greeted him with a hearty shout. Bob was sat in the same seat, drinking the same drink, and again reading the Bangkok Post as he had been on their previous meeting.

"A creature of habit, I see." John waved his hand around Bob's table.

"Oh yes, The Lowe is in his thinking mode, a couple of complex cases to solve."

John had begun to think there could be some mileage in this Bob Lowe; he had chatted with his editor and they were considering a weekly column in their magazine section entitled 'the view from the street', where an anonymous private investigator could briefly outline his cases and key issues. He raised this notion with Bob.

"What a marvellous idea, John! That magazine needs an injection of Boblowvian thought." Boblowvian. Bob had invented the term then and there. He was instantly enamoured with it.

They chatted about how this could work and Bob said it would be simply impossible for him to discuss, even covertly, any of his live cases. He would have to write 'as live' but about past and solved cases from the street. He wondered if starting in three to six months might be appropriate.

"Well at the moment it's just an idea, Bob." John realised he may need to dampen the roaring flames.

"But a fucking good one! Pardon my French! Lowe!" Bob mockingly slapped his hand and roared with laughter.

Lowe sat for an additional hour in the café, drinking copious amounts of water, and considering that he had saved at least five baht by doing so. He also managed to enjoy two rounds of free samples, a spinach croissant and a morsel of a muffin. "Utterly wonderful," he thanked the chap who had kindly delivered.

He strutted back to Daeng's. Tomorrow was tuk-tuk day, and he decided the best course of action was to apprehend the thief as he disembarked near the BTS with his tuk-tuk full of pork and/or drugs.

Bob crept quietly down the stairs at 4:50am, being careful not to wake Daeng. He was cutting it quite fine, but the tuk-tuk thief had never surfaced before 5:05 so he felt pretty safe. He took a left out of Daeng's house so he could walk the long way round, just to be sure that he didn't bump into the thief on his way. As he walked, Bob wondered if it was really fair to consider the chap a thief. He was returning the item each day. He vowed to check the dictionary for a full definition of a thief. He suspected there was a German word that would fit. The Germans were usually good for very specific words and he decided they may have one for a thief who stole an item regularly and returned it.

He verbalised some ideas he was brainstorming for a new word in English "Thieforer" or "Borrowief" – both rather uninspiring combinations of two words.

"Needs more work, Lowe."

He returned to a German theme. If the Germans didn't have such a word then he should create it. "Fluegenshaft!" he shouted. As he walked down the soi with his trademark loping gait he muttered, "Yep, let's catch this pesky fluegenshaft."

He managed to quickly nip into his favourite 7-Eleven, marvelling at the range of products and once again pondering Susie's ignorance. He treated himself to a custardy treat to go with his cappuccino and cheerily informed the young chap working there that the coffee was "basically as good as Starbucks. Aroy!"

Bob's enthusiastic shouting was a clear sign of his new positivity as his life continued on an upward trajectory.

He settled down on the steps by the Silom Centre and began to tuck into his custard bun, slurping noisily on his coffee. Inevitably a lump of gooey custard oozed out and dripped onto his shirt. "Oh, damn it, Lowe!" He fumbled around with his 7-Eleven napkin, leaving a residue of tissue detritus on his T-shirt. An inebriated drunk staggered by and stared at the comic scene "Bloody custard buns, old boy!" The drunk didn't react – he seemed British to Bob – but before he went too deep in his judging of this chap traipsing around drunk at five in the morning he remembered it wasn't long ago he was one of them. "New Lowe. New Lowe." He muttered his mantra to himself and surveyed the early morning scene in Silom.

It was still dark, and there was a building intensity in the atmosphere as the temperature was already stifling and the last residue of the night's business, typified by the drunk Brit, began to merge with the early morning food stalls setting up before one of Bangkok's busiest business zones fired into life. Bob continued to mutter, "Marvellous scene."

Some moments later the tuk-tuk pulled up and stopped by the BTS steps. "Right, Lowe, you're up!" He suddenly realised that he didn't have a clear plan of what he would say, but was confident he could wing it.

He greeted the young chap with a hello and instantly asked if he could speak English.

"Can, litten bit." The disinterested chap replied.

"Aha. Pork, eh? Moo grob." Bob eased his way into his stride. His strategy was to use his amiable style to get the guy onside.

"Khrap pom. My mother sell."

"Aha. She's your mother!"

The chap didn't feel the need to respond and Lowe was now intrigued. He instantly abandoned his strategy, realising he wasn't going to get much small talk.

"So. This tuk-tuk. Your mother's?" Lowe went in for the kill; the chap didn't reply.

"Well, it's not it's Khun Daeng's. You sir are a thief, or a thieforer or as the Germans might say a filthy flugenshaft. Kamoy khrap!"

On hearing the accusation of being a thief the young man replied. "I not thief. I come back every day. Pay one hundred baht."

Bob didn't quite know how to play this. He was expecting a denial. "Aha. So you admit it! Mai dee! Khun Daeng my friend."

The young man continued to focus on unloading the pork and setting up the table. Bob was searching for any evidence of drugs. He could only see pork.

"Sell only pork?" Bob felt in control of this.

"Not only."

"Aha! Got you! Here we go." Bob was getting excited.

The young man opened a bag of fried chicken wings and showed Bob.

"Bik gai tort! Delicious! Aroy!" Bob had lost his focus and began to get over enthusiastic about the

170

food.

The man smiled and handed Bob one to taste. He quickly devoured it. Bob asked the man his name.

"Nont Khrap."

Luckily Bob had made one advance plan, namely to ask Pat to be ready on the end of the phone to help him in this situation. Bob phoned her and waited patiently for Nont to finish unloading his produce.

He quickly updated Pat on the situation and handed Nont the phone. "It my friend."

Nont had an animated chat and at times there was some laughter. His mother strolled along, recognising Bob and smiled at him before asking him if he wanted fried pork.

"Yes, yes! Wonderful. Who wouldn't?"

This was all taking a strange turn. He was buying pork while the thief was chatting and joking with Pat on Bob's phone.

Eventually he handed Bob back his smartphone and Bob eagerly asked Pat for an update. "Right, Pat, spill the beans!"

All he could hear was hysterical laughing. "Bob! It so funny..."

"Stop your infernal giggling, this is important business. Professionalism, Pat. If I've told you once I've told you... well a few times. Professionalism. Is. The. Key."

It took Pat some time to fully compose herself. Eventually she managed to explain what was going on. Nont's mother had been selling fried pork on the street for years and years. Every day he drove her to her pitch with all the food items and tables. Recently his vehicle had broken down. He didn't have the parts to fix it, and he didn't want to admit to his mother that he didn't have enough money to repair it. So he told her it was taking some time, but that a friend had agreed to lend him the tuk-tuk. Thus every morning he borrowed the tuk-tuk and collected the pork and table to deliver to his mother's pitch.

She would walk there, and with all the produce sold would walk back just carrying the table.

It all made perfect sense. Bob was partly disappointed that it wasn't as exciting as he had thought, but also relieved that he didn't have a big drug case to deal with.

"Well, thank goodness he didn't know what I thought," a relieved Bob told Pat.

"He knows! That why he laugh so much." Pat began laughing again.

"Confidentiality, Pat! Friendship over!"

He arranged to meet up with Pat for an early dinner to discuss the next steps on this case, now that apparently he had solved it.

"Exactly as I expected of course, the drugs angle was always a secondary idea – one that us private investigators have to keep up our sleeves. I certainly didn't expect it to be true."

"Sure, Bob, of course." Pat did her best to sound sincere.

THIRTY

For Marjorie Dubshott the Lumpini Park Hotel was the crème de la crème of the venues for the BWBLS and she tried to ensure that they visited once a month in their venue rotations. She had enjoyed many wonderful evenings there during Humphrey's ambassadorial period and it therefore had a special place deep within her heart. There was a faded grandeur to the hotel that the nouveau riche just couldn't understand. Others always opted for the more opulent modern hotel chains with their slick ubiquitous feel. She arrived early as usual to set up for the ladies and wandered past the photos on the wall – an array of huge black and white images of some of the splendid occasions from over the years. She paused at her favourite. *His Royal Highness Prince Charles of Great Britain with Sir Humphrey and Lady Dubshott.* Prince Charles was laughing at something Marjorie had said and the photographer had captured the moment perfectly; Marjorie Dubshott relaxed and friendly with members of the British Royal Family. It had been a truly wonderful evening. She felt a deep sense of melancholy as she remembered her glory days. She sped on past the next photo *Chanatip and Gladys Suprawongse* and went to prepare the lobby area for their bridge and coffee morning. They would usually use the Orchid Room, but it had been booked by another function and Marjorie didn't want to miss out on their monthly visit to the Lumpini. She had arranged the money pot tucked in by a large tree in the corner of the raised mezzanine floor where they would have this week's session.

The Lumpini was also a perfect venue for Bob Lowe as it meant he could nip back home to Daeng's place and get a few hours' sleep and still be in good time to settle in at the Lumpini before the women arrived. He reviewed the morning's events in his mind and supposed that it was clear that the woman and her son weren't drug dealers, but then he considered that they were hardly going to admit it to a stranger on the street. He was feeling very much at home now at Daeng's and Daeng was finding Bob a very useful housemate. When Daeng left a dirty plate or glass in the sink, which he now did daily, Bob would inevitably wash it up. Bob got back to the house and found the remains of Daeng's breakfast in the sink. "Khun Daeng, what are you like!" Bob hollered as he quickly got to work on washing up. Bob had taught Daeng one of his favourite thrifty tricks – watering down washing up liquid. He would fill an empty washing up bottle no more than one-sixth full of liquid and then top up slowly with water. Daeng was impressed with some of Bob's money saving techniques. After a couple of hours resting Bob got himself settled on a table in the lobby lounge and sat reading the Bangkok Post with a clear view of the money pot.

The women started to arrive in dribs and drabs with no sign of Gladys, Bob had been warned that she always tended to arrive late, since she didn't play bridge, though in Marjorie's eyes she just wanted to make an entrance. Linda arrived and nodded at Marjorie; they had briefly discussed the previous evening how they would deal with the situation. Marjorie had suggested that they should keep it within the women's group and that obviously Gladys could no longer be a member after she had been exposed. For Marjorie, humiliating Gladys in front of the BWBLS was ample reward. Marjorie had begun to slowly harden her words with Linda. "I don't care that she's taking our money, but she's stealing from the charities too. Those poor orphans. She's stealing from them." Linda agreed that it was simply disgusting.

Bob looked quite a sight, in a full linen suit with a Panama hat and black shoes, he struggled his way through the Bangkok Post, and then began to make something of a scene of himself as he tried to fold the large pages neatly so he could read. Occasionally he would surreptitiously peer over the top of the paper to check he had a clear view of the women and their money pot. Marjorie found the whole scene quite comical, and she wondered whether she really needed this guy. But she explained to Linda that it would help to have an independent confirm what she already knew, and Bob Lowe, she felt, would be easy to convince of what she already knew. The card game started with little drama, a few giggles and squeals. Bob knew nothing about bridge but it seemed every so often the women were making academic errors, based on their comments. Marjorie glanced at the door regularly and when she did she would catch the eye of Bob, who twice nodded at her. Hardly inconspicuous. Eventually Gladys arrived making her grand entrance and Marjorie leapt from her chair.

"Gladys, darling! How wonderful to see you."

"Hello, Marjorie. Sorry I'm late."

Gladys was always late, so it incensed Marjorie that she would make a false show of apologising. Marjorie grabbed her by the arm, delicately helping her to walk to the payment bowl. Bob put down his paper and was quite obviously carefully watching the scene. Linda Taylor was also glancing from her vantage point, playing bridge.

The two ladies chatted and Bob couldn't hear what was being said from this distance. He tried to use his smartphone to zoom in, but it wasn't much help. Marjorie and Gladys crowded over the bowl as Gladys removed her purse from her handbag.

"Blast, move, Marjorie!" Bob muttered to himself. He couldn't get a clear view of the bowl as Marjorie and Gladys were both blocking his eye line. After some moments they turned back in Bob's direction. Gladys put down her handbag and Marjorie returned to her bridge game. Bob was frustrated, but it was clearly the client's fault. It wasn't clear what was going on. A moment later his phone buzzed with a message from Marjorie, *Did you see her stuff those notes quickly into her bag?* Bob replied, *Negative, view obscured.*

He got up and walked through the women's tables and, pretending he was just casually strolling through the hotel, he peered down at Gladys's handbag which was placed on a spare chair and he could indeed see a few one thousand-baht notes at the top of the handbag. He took out his smartphone and while pretending to take a photo of the hotel lobby he quickly snapped a photo of the offending handbag.

He continued to walk through the lobby, while looking around with his hand on his chin at times. It was as if he had been asked to do a bad act of a private detective going undercover and pretending to not be looking at what he was obviously looking at.

Marjorie and Linda trotted after Bob and got into an animated conversation. "So, did you confirm she had the money?" Marjorie asked.

"It would appear that way, yes." Bob showed the women the photo.

Linda squealed. "Oh, it's too awful. Gladys, a thief." They continued their conversation and Bob explained to them that for an investigator like him it was vitally important that he corroborated the evidence.

"Can you use this venue again next week? I'd like to have a repeat, to confirm." Bob tried to convey an air of confidence. Linda and Marjorie agreed it was an excellent idea.

They BWBLS members returned to their game where most of the others hadn't even noticed the two chatting with the strangely attired, but not quite dapper, British chap.

Bob sat down back in the same seat and carefully looked around the venue. Something wasn't adding up for him. He made a few notes and this time formulated a clear plan of action. He was confident that he could bring this case to a conclusion the next time they met.

THIRTY ONE

"It's margarita o'clock, Pat!" Bob slurped enthusiastically from the strawberry margarita that he had poured from the large jug, spilling some down the sides of the glass.

"When in Mexico, my dear!" Bob bizarrely winked at Pat as he said this, as if it had some deeper meaning.

"Delicious!" Pat wasn't really one to enjoy the delights of alcoholic imbibing, but a fruity cocktail was an exception for her.

Pat explained to Bob that it was clear Nont was embarrassed, about losing his job, not being able to repair the truck and therefore not being able to drive his mum to her work pitch each day.

Pat was adamant that Bob's business should be about helping people become better human beings, helping them to do the right thing, "put the world on a good path" as she like to state it.

"Zen Lowe… you may be on to something here, young Pat." Lowe did his best 'wistful Lowe' act as he looked out around the Mexican restaurant.

"I will speak with Nont, tell him to ask Khun Daeng if he can hire the tuk-tuk each day." Pat got straight to the point.

"Good Lord, Pat, no, no, no. If he does that, Daeng will know he is the tuk-tuk thief. You'll cause quite a kerfuffle. Leave this to the professional."

"He not say anything. I know men like Daeng." Pat went on to express her thoughts to Bob. Of course, both men would know the truth, but it would remain unsaid and an outcome that was of mutual benefit could result, in the right way. On this occasion he chose not to argue and to listen intently. When it came to matters of Thai culture and foibles, at least he recognised Pat's greater knowledge and expertise.

They thrashed out a plan. He would inform Daeng the case was closed, the tuk-tuk would no longer be stolen, but for reasons of confidentiality he could not explain how and why. His official recommendation was that this was not a matter for police involvement. Daeng would of course agree. He certainly could do without the hassle of officialdom. Or in the words of the Brit, "Trust the Lowe."

For the next week or so the tuk-tuk should remain, 'unstolen' to prove the case was solved, then Nont could approach Daeng about borrowing the tuk-tuk.

"It's a superb plan, Pat, but there is one small detail. This is why you are merely my assistant and not a PI, my dear. What pray will Nont do for the next week?" Bob sat back, arms folded as if he were some sort of smug savant.

Pat smiled. "What you doing at five tomorrow morning, Bob?"

And so it was that at five the following morning

Pat, Bob and Nont, each with four or five big plastic bags full of pork, shuffled their way down the soi to Nont's mother's pitch. The sweat began to pour down Bob's face and with his hands weighed down by fried pork he could do nothing to stop the sweat dripping into his eyes. It reminded him of a horrendous incident in Lampang one year. Bob had visited during the hottest time of the year. "Up to the cooler northern climes," he had informed friends, neglecting to realise that those cooler northern areas were much hotter in the summer months! In the height of the daytime sun, with the thermometer comfortably exceeding forty degrees he'd stumbled around with bags of heavy shopping. His sweat was so salty that he'd felt a stinging in his eyes affecting his vision and having avoided a couple of cars he'd collided with a, fortunately slow moving, motorbike. His bag of fruit had flown across the road, dragon fruit, pomelo, and mangoes creating a Lowe fruit cocktail in the middle of a busy Lampang intersection. Momentarily, Lowe had been relieved as he then had a spare hand to wipe his brow, before it dawned on him that he'd lost a few hundred baht's worth of fruit. The next day he invested in a 1980s Bjorn Borg style headband.

"I'll Borg it up tomorrow, Pat," Bob cheerily stated. This was one nonsensical comment that Pat chose to ignore, she had no idea what he was talking about but didn't feel she needed to know.

THIRTY TWO

Bob had been binge reading and binge watching any detective books and TV series he could. Documentaries, fiction, even some of the more comic-satire variety. He was learning his trade slowly but surely and it was certainly noticeable that he was becoming more perceptive. Bob was aware of it himself, picking up on signs and signals. He kept being uncannily right about little things. It was unnerving. This was indeed 'New Lowe'. What next he pondered? Should he get himself a slick designer suit? Shades?

"Easy, Lowe." He grimaced, as he realised he was letting his mind wander and things could be in danger of getting out of hand. He was certain he had picked up on some strange things at 'The Lumpini' during the ladies bridge session and he was convinced he was right. He had discussed with Marjorie the need to repeat the same the following week.

"If you want me to apprehend this Gladys chap, we need to do a controlled experiment. Let's just say I am on to the old girl," Lowe confidently informed Marjorie Dubshott.

"Chap or chapess? Can one say chapess? Can a woman be a chap? If not, why?" Marjorie decided to ignore this nugget of Lowe-speak.

Marjorie phoned her dear friend John Albertson.

"Hello, Marjorie, got a scoop for me?" Albertson asked with a hint of mischief in his voice.

"Oh, John, don't be so vulgar! You know very well I would never want to embarrass Gladys. She is a Bangkok legend after all." Marjorie got her sarcastic tone perfect, a lifetime of experience.

"Of course, of course, what was I thinking."

"Anyway, John. We will be having our weekly BWBLS meeting this Thursday at the Lumpini."

"I see, so you mean..." John began to speak in a more serious tone before Marjorie cut him off.

"I mean nothing, just chatting you know. Anyway toodle pip, must dash. We must do lunch sometime."

Lowe donned the same attire he had done on the previous week's visit to the Lumpini and sat in the exact same spot. Marjorie had set things up as she had the previous week, with the money pot in the same location. Bob surveyed the scene. "Hmmm, just as I suspected." He sent a couple of text messages and got ready to solve this case.

"Judgement day!" he declared, to the bemusement of the couple sat on the table next to him.

"Apologies, just thinking out loud." He felt the need to try and explain, but the couple ignored him and carried on chatting.

Just as on the previous week the bridge players

began playing bridge before Gladys had arrived, and she made her entrance at about ten thirty, half an hour into the game. The identical routine played out, confirming Bob's suspicions.

Marjorie returned to her game. *Confirm the money is in the bag, and then we will have to expose her, tactfully,* she texted Bob.

Bob looked up and nodded to Marjorie, before replying, *I have everything I need. Case solved. Lowe does it again.* He noticed Marjorie chuckle when she read the message.

Marjorie replied, *We need to expose her, please take a photo of the bag this minute.*

Bob ignored the text and sat patiently.

Marjorie began to grow frustrated. *DO NOT be so impertinent, I AM NOT paying you to sit and sip coffee. Take a photo of the money in the top of the bag NOW!*

Again Bob glanced at the text and chose to ignore it. She made an elementary mistake in the card game, costing her crucial points and kept looking up at Bob Lowe, who kept on pretending he hadn't noticed.

She got up and walked over to pour herself a coffee. "AAAAHHH!" she screamed loudly, everyone turning to look at her.

"Gladys! How could you!? Ladies, we have a thief in our midst. Gladys has been stealing from the money. I've suspected for weeks and today I saw her." Marjorie sounded distressed.

Gladys looked up. "Have you taken leave of your senses, Marjorie? Someone get her a glass of water." Gladys was genuinely slightly concerned for Marjorie after this strange outburst.

"Don't play the innocent with me. How do you explain four thousand baht sitting at the top of your bag, with a little red dot in the corner of each? Caught you red-handed!" Marjorie had taken on a more acidic tone.

Gladys just looked utterly bemused. The women were all shocked. Marjorie took the opportunity to pounce. "Yes, you play this perfect role, but you've never fooled me. All this nonsense, all on the back of your husband – who is a crook by the way. You are nothing, Gladys, and now I move to throw you out of the BWBLS in utter shame."

John Albertson was watching with incredulous excitement and furiously taking notes. A more modern journalist would have been filming for a YouTube video, but John chose to take notes in shorthand.

At that moment, Bob stood and walked towards Marjorie.

"Ah, thanks, Bob. This is a private detective who I, with great regret I might add, had to employ to catch this disgusting thief. Bob, please confirm what you have witnessed." Marjorie waved her arm to signify the floor was now Bob's.

"Marjorie, I think perhaps we should go somewhere quiet." Bob was trying to be sympathetic.

"Too late for that, Bob. We have all seen what has happened. Can you confirm these thousand-baht-notes are from the Bangkok Women's pot?" Marjorie was indignant.

"Confirmed, Marjorie..."

There was an audible gasp from the women.

"Confirmed. Did you hear that, ladies? Gladys Suprawongse is a nasty thief." Marjorie had some spittle forming in the edge of her mouth as she spoke.

Bob tried again to take a compassionate approach.

"I really think we should sort this out in private, Marjorie."

Marjorie turned her vitriol on Bob. "Oh, you pathetic man. I have paid you handsomely to do a job now do as I have told you! How dare you try to tell me what to do. Impertinence. Tell these women what has been going on!" she screamed.

"Very well. Ladies, I am indeed Bob Lowe. Bangkok's finest farang investigator, in my opinion. Of course I can't claim for any independent verification of said fact, as of yet."

"Oh, for the love of God will you just get on with it."

"I have indeed seen that cash from the money pot is now in the bag of Gladys Suprawongse and I am afraid I did notice the very same last week."

"Oh for goodness sake, what on earth is all this." Gladys had barely spoken but she really was getting curious and now slightly irritated by this ridiculous chain of events.

Bob nodded his head towards Gladys. "Khunying Gladys, I am sorry to have to involve you..."

"Sorry?!" Marjorie yelled. "She's a common thief. We should call the police, frankly."

"Marjorie, that won't be necessary. Yes I am indeed sorry, Gladys, as you are entirely innocent of any wrong doing," Bob said confidently.

"Oh for pity's sake, Bob, you have just confirmed the ugly truth. What are you saying? She didn't know what she was doing? The old cow ain't senile yet!" Marjorie laughed an aggressive and evil laugh.

"I am saying no such thing. Khun Daeng, please come here." Bob waved to Khun Daeng who was sitting quietly at the other side of the lobby.

"I am saying Gladys had no idea what *you* were doing, Marjorie Dubshott." Bob gave her a smug grin.

"I believe my trusted colleague, Khun Daeng has caught the whole episode on video. I thought it odd last week, Marjorie, that you deliberately blocked my line of sight. Trying to outfox the Lowe may be a bold move but it ultimately ends in failure, as indeed it would for anyone else. I am to Bangkok what Hercule Poirot was to, well wherever Poirot was from. Was it Belgium?"

He held the smartphone that Daeng handed to him and played a video; it clearly showed with great clarity that as Marjorie went to greet Gladys and help her to the money pot she then surreptitiously placed a handful of notes into the top of her handbag.

"That, madam, is what we call 'bang to rights'. Underestimate The Lowe at your peril."

Marjorie sat down, speechless. Speechless and shell-shocked. The women gathered around Gladys who was looking equally bewildered.

Linda Foxsmith-Taylor stood up. "I hereby call an emergency vote of the BWBLS. All those in favour of Marjorie Dubshott's lifetime ban from the BWBLS please raise your hand and say aye'"

All the hands went up, with the exception of Gladys who was too upset.

Bob raised his hand enthusiastically, before realising that he wasn't entitled to and apologetically put it back down.

"Let the record show that, as of now, Marjorie Dubshott is persona non grata. Please leave the BWBLS."

Gladys spoke. "All those in favour of Linda Foxsmith-Taylor's immediate election as acting chair of the BWBLS please raise your hand and say aye."

The same was repeated; this time Gladys raised her hand and an embarrassed Bob apologised again for his previous attempt to vote "Electoral fraud? Not on The Lowe's watch. Marjorie stood and walked out in floods of tears.

John Albertson frantically scribbled in his notebook and strolled over to Bob. "We must meet for a glass of wine and a chat about your work."

Bob did a little jig in a moment of immense pride with his head theatrically raised.

He walked over to Khun Daeng, shook his hand and patted him on the back enthusiastically.

"Just another day for Bob Lowe, my dear old thing."

THIRTY THREE

Bob finally got the chance to arrange his catch-up with Khun Pun, and they agreed to meet up at Mints Bar. Bob was genuinely finding it hard to schedule everything as he had so much going on. He was initially slightly concerned when he got the message from the police sergeant but Mint had put his mind at ease.

"He think maybe you help each other, no problem," Mint had informed Bob earlier that week.

"Of course. Makes sense, two law enforcement officers working together. Classic Pun, he'll have been hearing about my investigative skills, no doubt." Bob was talking to himself now as Mint had moved off to take orders from another table. He put up the posters to detail the return of Avi Shielmann and the special beer promotion for the night. Mint had told Bob she would get a little stage set up and after Avi's act they could have a karaoke night. She had even agreed to pay a cut of any profits, over a certain amount, on beer promotion. Another avenue opening up for his fledgling business.

Since solving the Gladys case he had been musing over how to deal with the Pim and Brian business. He had broken the news to Pim of Brian's philandering ways, and he'd laid it on pretty thick. Much to his surprise, Pim didn't seem too disappointed. Things had been going well with Werner and she had already planned she would break up with Brian in the next few weeks.

Bob was happy for Pim, but he wasn't happy that this should be the end of it.

"It's utterly sickening, Nong Pat, these animals behaving in this way." Bob was furious as he talked it over with Pat over lunch that day.

"I wonder if there is anything Khun Pun can do for me?" Bob mused as Pat focused on her noodle soup. She knew Bob liked to talk and talk to get into his flow and she knew she just needed to prod him in the right direction for him to reach a decision. The correct decision – Pat's decision.

She was pleasantly surprised and certainly noted the irony of Bob's comments. She had of course become aware that Bob had very much 'played the Nana scene' back in the day, and now here he was appalled at what was really run of the mill antics for these types of men.

Bob talked and talked, with Pat adding things like 'maybe' and 'good idea' as Bob rambled on.

Eventually Pat reminded Bob, "You do know that prostitution is illegal in Thailand..."

"Nong Pat, you little beauty! You've done it again! Of course. I can simply arrange for him to be met by some of Bangkok's friendliest boys in brown."

Bob began to daydream; his own version of

vigilante justice. Maybe he could have Brian beaten up, money stolen, or simply fined by the police. Arrested? All three? The possibilities were rushing around in his head.

"That filthy scumbag." Noodles slurped out of his mouth as he spoke.

"Why don't I come with you to meet Khun Pun?" Pat felt this was a reasonable request as she was now a key part of Bob's operation.

"Now, now, Pat, with all due respect, soi Nana is not really the place for a young lady such as yourself."

Bob genuinely felt it wasn't an appropriate environment for Pat, but he also had a great fear of his two different worlds colliding. The Bob who was friendly with Pat and had been a dedicated teacher and the Bob who was a slobbering drunk picking up prostitutes in Nana. He didn't want Pat to think worse of him. Perhaps in time, but he still didn't feel comfortable about it.

Pat didn't press the issue, and Bob explained that of course in the fullness of time one of his junior executive investigators would be required to attend such meetings. He realised she would be very useful for him to navigate both linguistic and cultural confusions that may arise.

As soon as Pun walked in, Bob stood and placed his hands together wai-ing the policeman with great respect. It had the desired effect and Pun was happy to see Bob. Bob instantly ordered two beers and asked Mint for the menu.

"You're looking marvellously well, Khun Pun, oh to be a youngster like you again!" Bob was developing his skills as an old charmer.

With a big grin on his face, Pun excitedly told Bob

he was in fact forty-eight years old, older than Bob himself.

"Utterly absurd!"

Whilst it may have been true that Pun looked young for his age, it was unmistakably true that Bob looked much older than his early forties. Most would place Bob at around fifty, but one could be forgiven for edging a prediction up towards sixty. Bob had grown accustomed to the mocking and had decided his best strategy was to embrace his looks.

"Doctors want to study me, I must hold all the answers to ageing, since I'm doing it so well!"

Pun chuckled. "No, no. You also young man, like me." Bob took Pun at face value, even if he realised he probably wasn't sincere.

"You are too kind, Pun!"

They enjoyed a quick and casual catch-up, with Bob almost right on most of his facts, or wrong on most facts if one wanted to take a slightly harsher approach. Bob was becoming a 'glass half full man' so he preferred to think of his almost right being accurate enough.

"You have two daughters, yes?" Bob enquired.

"No, just one."

"Yes, of course, she goes to that top Thai school in Asok, I think I am right in saying." Bob was almost certain of this one.

"No, she goes to international school, she doing very well."

This pattern continued for some time with Bob blustering his way through with many a "Yes, of course, I remember now." Bob made a mental note that he needed to keep notes about these sorts of things. He then momentarily pondered about how he would note that he had made a mental note. Oh the complexities of the world of New Lowe.

"So, Bob, what's all this I hear about your unlicensed private detective business…?" Pun very subtly focused on the word unlicensed.

Bob momentarily froze. He hadn't even thought about this angle at all. He was now of course technically working illegally in Thailand and about to discuss just that matter with a policeman, and a senior one no less.

"Er. Business? What?" Bob's dreadful bluffing was the best attempt he could make at stalling for some time.

"Lor len, Bob, just joking." Pun took another swig of his beer and laughed out loud.

"Pun! You old so and so! You had The Lowe scared there for a split second, just a split second mind. Almost imperceptible."

Bob went on to explain the low-key nature of his business, but also explained how Pun might be able to help, and how it could be mutually beneficial. "Symbiosis, Khun Pun. Symbiosis."

"I can fix bad farang. You give me name, picture, and place. My boys will arrange." Pun spoke reasonable English, with a slight American twang to it. Bob had always been fascinated by Pun and wondering what his story was. They had only ever been bar acquaintances so Bob had never felt able to pry for details.

They discussed an informal business arrangement. While officially of course, Pun wanted to clear the streets of drugs and the major dealers, he was also acutely aware that if this ever succeeded it would be financially disadvantageous for him and his colleagues. He preferred to focus on the idea of knowledge giving him increased power. Bob could play a crucial role. Some of the core income generation for the boys in brown were the classic drunk foreigners caught in possession of weed, cocaine, or crystal methamphetamine (ya ice). They'd quickly and happily hand over ten to twenty thousand baht to avoid an arrest and the possibility of a lengthy prison sentence.

Bob informed Pun that there was no question he could pass on some intel to that effect. Bob also pitched the idea of some small easy cash jobs. He would inform Pun of some cheating scoundrels, and the police could stop them when using a prostitute or sex service, and fine them a few thousand to avoid arrest.

Pun carefully explained to Bob that one didn't want to upset the careful dynamic that existed in the city with the sex trade, but he agreed he could help Bob out on occasions, as a favour. They agreed Pun would pay an informal ten per cent 'finder's fee' to Bob for any successful fines the police managed to accrue.

"Another beer for Khun Pun, Nong Mint!" Bob barked his orders and got a steely glare from Mint.

"Sorry, I mean when you've got a moment, sorry. Sorry!"

He backtracked in classic Lowe fumbling style.

"This really is a magnificent city, Khun Pun. This afternoon I was in one of the finest shopping malls in the world. Now I'm sat on this unique street drinking with an esteemed law enforcement officer like your good self. What a world we live in, Khun Pun. What a world."

Bob was beginning to get misty eyed – Bangkok could do that to him at times. Over the years he'd gone through many emotions with Bangkok; love, hate, frustration, obsession even. There were times when he really felt Bangkok wasn't a healthy place for him to live with his prior addictions to the sex, booze and drugs that were so easily accessible. However, he just couldn't imagine living anywhere else.

"I live here all my life, Bob. As children I lived near to Lad Phrao. It was a very, very quiet place then. My father, he remember the rice paddies. In Lad Phrao!"

"Marvellous. Lad Phrao. Utterly marvellous."

They sat in silence for some moments before Bob explained all the details of the Brian situation and how he just wanted to see things work out for Pim.

"Leave that with me, Bob."

They shook hands and Bob sat back, catching Mint's eye, more politely this time, and signifying that one more beer would suit him very well.

THIRTY FOUR

Pim had made the decision about Brian even before Bob confirmed her suspicions, but she was pleased to have the truth established by the work of an expert. She thanked Bob profusely and paid him an additional tip for his work. It amused both of them, here was Pim, an ex-bar girl who Bob had once bar-fined, now paying Bob, and technically from Brian's bank account too. Pim had realised she must have been right about Brian by the simple fact that she had started developing strong feelings for Werner. Such was Pim's logic, but it made perfect sense to her. The idea of having Bob spy on Werner was ludicrous and preposterous to her, not to mention totally unnecessary. However, she was touched that Bob had offered. He seemed to genuinely care about her welfare; another clear sign to her that things were starting to look up in life, finally. She had first met Werner about a year earlier. He was in Bangkok on holiday with some friends, all in their late fifties and all seemingly either recently divorced or never married. She could tell instantly that Werner was attracted to her. So she began to focus her attention and energy on him thinking he was a potential customer, and at the very least an easy way to accrue some commissions from lady-drinks. Like many, Pim was starting to grow weary of the bar scene. She didn't hate it quite in the way some of her friends did but the constant need to give platitudes to so many pathetic men quickly grew tiresome. She had dated men before from the bars, but it had never worked out. She knew deep down that it was never going to either, but still so many tried. Yes, there were a handful of girls she'd known who successfully navigated their path from bar girl to happily married woman, but those few were the exceptions. Most of the time they'd be back working the bars – in some cases it was only a matter of weeks, in others years, but invariably the result was the same. It never worked out as they had dreamed and frankly life as a hooker was easier and better. The ones who managed to emigrate out of Thailand with their guys stood a better chance, but ultimately the sort of men who bought a woman in a bar just weren't the sort to settle down to a quiet married life. Some of them simply wanted an 'easy' girlfriend for the year or so they worked in Thailand.

Pim's friends were amused that Werner hadn't wanted to have sex with her and they joked about what was wrong with him. They had arranged a date that she just assumed was the standard sort of date men usually wanted from her. She had initially found it slightly awkward when they went for dinner in a nice Thai restaurant. She wasn't expecting that. Her friends had reminded her that even if Werner paid for dinner it was still costing her money. She wasn't working, so she was losing money and he wasn't paying any bar fine. 'Don't be fooled into becoming a 'friend' to one of these losers,' was a line her friends often delivered to her, from bitter experience. Pim was convinced that Werner was genuinely a different sort of guy, a softer soul. His friends had all hooked up with girls and had headed for a few days in Pattaya. Werner opted to stay in Bangkok because he wanted to spend more time getting to know Pim, and trying to pick up some more Thai phrases. After his holiday was over he had indeed kept in touch via WhatsApp, but she was still surprised when he told her he wanted to retire in Thailand. She had decided to take a risk, take the bull by the horns and tell Werner she wanted to be with him, as his girlfriend. She knew a shy guy like him needed her to take the lead, and he was delighted at the suggestion. She felt no guilt at leaving Brian. She had never really been into him but had been encouraged to give it a go by her friends. Playing the game and testing the waters until you find the right one was never really her thing, but she figured she had tried and failed at playing this game and now it was time to get out.

She had planned things with Bob on a day that Brian had told her he'd be late home from work. Lowe had gone over at lunchtime and helped her with her few suitcases, and some of the ornaments from the house that she had picked out on their shopping trips. Werner had seemed quite keen to live a quiet life away from the bright lights and big city so she was busy making plans to move back to Korat and live with Werner there.

An hour later Bob waved goodbye to Pim having

helped her into Werner's condo. As he left he texted Pun with some of the details for later. Bob had already supplied some names and information to Pun that led to some easy street payments so he had happily agreed to do Bob a favour and deal with this Brian.

Later that evening two of Bangkok's finest officers greeted Brian when he walked out of a massage parlour, the one near Ratchada that Bob had informed them about.

"You pay sex? Illegal. We arrest you."

"You fucking what, mate?" Without thinking things through Brian immediately took on his typically aggressive tone. A big mistake.

"We hear many bad things. Your girl Pim she already go away with better man."

Hearing the name of his girlfriend shocked Brian. This was not a normal situation he quickly realised.

"Bangkok not need you. Go home to America."

Bob had advised the police to use this line and it worked perfectly. Brian lurched back into his anger mode. "You calling me a fucking yank, you dozy Thai cunt."

Brian was only digging his hole deeper. Eventually he was fortunate enough to be allowed to 'agree' to a fee of fifteen thousand baht to avoid charges of soliciting sex, verbal assault of an officer, and resisting arrest.

The officers informed him that he should never try to contact Pim again, and if they ever had complaints about his disrespectful behaviour again they'd make a quick call to immigration and have him deported, forever.

The next evening Bob 'bumped' into Brian in a bar

on Soi Nana. Brian seemed perfectly normal, drinking and laughing with his mates.

"Ah, Brian, I've been looking for you, got an update for you on…"

Brian interrupted, "Save your breath, mate. I dumped that useless bitch a few days ago. Just not up to my standards." He laughed with his mates as he said it.

This time Bob wasn't furious. He was more amused. He knew just how humiliated Brian had been and here he was having to create this story for his friends. Bob knew what he must have been feeling inside though and that was victory enough.

"Oh, I see. Well I guess my services are no longer required. Best of British and all that, old bean."

Brian gave Bob a disinterested look and Bob continued on his merry way. He stopped off at a 7-Eleven on the way home to pick up a bottle of Sang Som for a quiet drink back at the house with Khun Daeng and sent him a text, *Get the ice on ice. I've bought us a bottle of Sang Som old boy!*

THIRTY FIVE

Bob was very lucky that Avi seemed to be the only person he knew without a Facebook profile. Lucky because Facebook had quickly become Bob's only strategy in his attempts to find Mo Razzaq, of disco fame. If Avi just used Facebook he'd probably be able to do as good a job as Bob was doing. All avenues had proved fruitless. Bob was amazed to discover the Embassy of Pakistan was on Soi Sukhumvit 3, a mere stone's throw from the Nana bars he regularly frequented. He had decided to pop in there one afternoon before going for a few drinks. He confidently approached the desk and informed them that he was trying to locate a Pakistani citizen. Initially he had been encouraged by the response he got. "Most Pakistani nationals are registered with us, so there may be a way we can pass on a message."

"Ah. No. Well you see, this chap, Mo Razzaq, perhaps you know him? Disco dancer, they say the finest ever to come out of Pakistan. Well you see he's not in Bangkok." As Bob spoke he began to become aware that this probably wasn't going to work. He could see the official immediately begin to lose interest, or start to consider that Bob was just another of Bangkok's fruitcakes.

"So where is he do you think?" he added out of politeness more than anything else.

"Last seen in Tokyo, 1983. I should add we are talking about a disco dancer of some repute, the quality of his moves, well, superb." It was as if Bob thought this would lead to the penny suddenly dropping, 'Oh, *that* Mo Razzaq.' Alas not. "I don't think we can help you, sir." As he spoke he glanced at the next customer in line, as a hint to Bob.

"Well would His Excellency the Pakistani ambassador be available, he may have some contacts." Eventually they managed to move Bob on, but not until after he had tried to name drop his tenuous connection to the late Humphrey Dubshott. Bob insisted on leaving his card so they could call him if they had any ideas on how to help.

He texted Avi. *I've got some of my contacts at the Pakistani Embassy on the case. Luckily I know the former British Ambassador's wife. She owes me a favour. Regards, Bob Lowe (PI).*

Later that same day Bob began to join lots of Pakistani and dancing groups on Facebook. Posting a picture of the great Mo from his dancing heyday. Bob had paused the YouTube video clip and then taken a photo with his phone. The quality was poor to fair, and Mo couldn't really be seen that clearly. He was amazed at how quickly things began to happen and he cursed himself for not trying this on day one. He got plenty of messages, most utter nonsense or trying to sell him something. Eventually he got a very simple message. *I'm Mo Razzaq, the disco dancer. Who are you?*

Bob was thunderstruck and very excited that he had actually cracked the case. Another! This one all by himself and genuinely really cracked. He had found Mo Razzaq! He had found a man in Pakistan with the only clue he had being a reference to 1980s disco. Bob noticed Mo didn't describe himself as an ex-disco dancer. He considered it must be rather like being an alcoholic perhaps, once disco was in your blood it never left. He chatted with Mo over a number of days, filling him in on exactly what was going on.

In consultation with Pat, Bob had decided to wait until Avi had finished his disco comeback night at Mints before hitting him with the incredible news. He didn't feel it was fair to Avi to unsettle him before the big night.

Pat had become a regular visitor to Daeng's house just off Soi Pipat. Daeng was enjoying the noise and life being back in the house. He especially liked it when Pat arrived with bags of food. It reminded him of Ploy.

"Khaw man gai, Daeng!"

At that Daeng had shimmied down the stairs with a fleet of foot that belied his years, though still relatively slow. Pat and Bob would lay out all the food and plates and they'd excitedly tuck into their food and discuss any updates on Bob's cases. Thai food was like that, even an old man like Daeng would get as excited as a child when his favourite dishes were presented.

"Oh, we have one more surprise…" As Pat spoke she revealed small plastic bags containing a favourite dessert of Daeng's; taro balls in hot coconut milk.

Daeng expressed his delight and looked at Bob. "You should marry this one!"

Bob blushed profusely before joining his friends in laughter.

The following evening Bob sat with Avi enjoying a pre-show drink.

"I'm really feeling nervous. It's been a long time."

"Balderdash. I saw you dance just last week," Bob reminded Avi in an attempt to allay his fears.

"That was just random. There are posters for this." There was a look of panic across Avi's face. Was he really doing this?

Bob remained confident. "That's why we are starting in Mints. Low-key re-launch of the great Avi Shielmann. This will be the best event in here for years."

The two men sat quietly as the bar began to fill up. Another busy night down Nana with all its usual drama and energy. Bob looked around and made his snap judgement on the night's clientele. A few of them he knew of course, fellow regulars. The rest he felt were easy to size up. This was one skill Bob genuinely did have. Over the years in Bangkok he had seen it all. He had seen all the behaviours, characters, and personalities. He could instantly assess a person in this part of town. He could see it in their eyes and body language. The ones who were experienced and therefore knew how to behave with a bit of respect, were easily spotted.

In one corner he saw a group of younger, cocky types. Just the sort Bob didn't like. His years of chatting with bar girls had taught him that the girls didn't much like these loud, brash characters either.

They thought they were *it*. They were nothing. The joke was on them.

"Not long now, Avi. This is the moment. *The moment!*"

"Don't make me any more nervous!"

There was technically a small dance floor in Mints, but people rarely actually danced on it. Mints wasn't really that sort of place. A couple of big posters had been put up in the corner to announce the imminent return of the eminent Avi Shielmann. Most drinkers in the bar hadn't even noticed. It was pretty unlikely the appearance of Avi was drawing the crowds.

Avi went into the little private room behind the bar to get changed. When he gave Bob the signal that he was ready, Bob stood up and took a microphone from Mint.

"Good evening, Mints!" Bob expected a huge roar, but what he got was at best muted. A couple of claps and the odd whistle.

"Some of you may know me as plain old Bob Lowe."

"Who the fuck are you, mate?" a random drunk heckled him, much to the amusement of a few others.

"Ah, yes, very good. Well tonight I am Bob Lowe – disco promoter. Yes, D.I.S.C.O. I give you something very special. The greatest disco dancer ever to perform here in Mints. Former world championship star. Ladies and gents. I give you Avi Shielmann!"

Mic drop. Literally, not for effect, Bob fumbled and dropped the mic. He was grappling on the floor as Avi entered and the Ottawan classic *D.I.S.C.O* started to play.

Avi strutted out with all the attitude of his younger

days. He wore an outrageous gold jumpsuit with silver sparkles. His chest hair was visible as was his chain. His hips gyrated from side to side. His hands pointed at random people in the audience.

The crowd at Mints roared, partly in humour, partly out of their sheer drunkenness. Within a few moments they were voicing their approval – they were genuinely impressed. Avi certainly had the moves for a man of his age and he knew how to get the crowd involved. For more than ten minutes Avi performed with all the gusto and energy of the disco superstar Bob had said he once was. He was in the moment. Adrenaline rushed through his body. Later he would tell Bob he had no memory of the performance at all. It just happened. It was bizarre, it was unique, and the Mints' crowd loved it.

When it was all over, an exhausted and emotional Avi slumped back down in his chair opposite Bob. During the course of the evening Avi got a lot of compliments from people walking by his table. "Awesome, mate," was a typical reaction.

He was overcome with emotion, tears welling in his eyes. "I can't thank you enough. I haven't had this feeling in years. I'm back. Avi Shielmann is back."

Bob let that hang in the air for a few moments. "If anyone can, Bob Lowe can. That's not all either. I've found Mo Razzaq." Avi just looked at Bob, and very slowly Bob could detect the tears in his eyes increasing in volume. It had been quite a night.

Over the course of the next few weeks the Bangkok heat began to rise, the cooler comfort of January but a distant memory. Bob looked back fondly as he often did. "January was but an English

205

summer's morn. Oh the joys. No sweating at all."
Werner and Pim both smiled at him. They had invited
the clumsy Brit out for lunch to thank him and
Werner had chosen his favourite German restaurant
in town. "This food it really remind me a lot of my
childhood. Good home cooked meals," he informed
Bob who was busy grappling with an enormous piece
of pork knuckle.

"Well it is delicious, but a confounded nuisance.
One needs a sharper knife." Bob had noticed a
difference in Pim. He considered that this must be
what happiness looked like. He had never
contemplated before that Pim didn't look happy, but
with hindsight he could see the difference. There was
a relaxed air about her. The way she sat. The way she
smiled. It was all natural. This really was remarkable.
As a fully-fledged cynic Bob liked to mock the idea of
couples being happy. This time he couldn't argue. He
could see it. "I must say you do make an utterly
splendid couple. Genuinely so. I couldn't be happier."
The couple held hands and smiled back at Bob.

His business was really bearing fruit and he
noticed that he was uplifted. Seeing other people so
happy and so grateful because of his work, Bob
Lowe's efforts gave him a warm feeling! It was
remarkable. He had stumbled upon something. Work
he enjoyed, but work that was also rewarding. After
lunch with Werner and Pim, he met Avi at Mints for
'one quick beer'. The Swedish-Israeli insisted on
paying. It was the least he could do. Thanks to the
efforts of Bob Lowe PI he was back in touch with his
oldest and dearest friend. They had traded a few
emails, Avi had apologised for his indiscretions of the

past, and they'd moved on. They updated each other on their lives and Mo had sent Avi pictures of his children, now both adults. Avi had missed so much of his friend's life. They began to Skype call – quite an emotional moment, seeing and hearing his old friend. They quickly seemed to slot back into their old friendship, like it was still the early 1980s. The same in jokes. Laughing over the same memories. Avi shared his disco comeback with his friend who was delighted for him and they discussed a reunion, perhaps in Bangkok. Maybe they would dance again to roars from the crowd. Life was good and one unconventional, often drunk Brit was to thank for it.

THIRTY SIX

One quiet Saturday morning, Bob sat out the front of the small house just off Soi Pipat drinking a morning coffee with Daeng and Nat. Bob had now joined the routine that the two older men had had for years. Conversation didn't flow smoothly, at least the conversation Bob tried to take part in didn't flow smoothly, but even in the short time he had been living with Daeng they had both managed to improve their language skills.

"Superb coffee as ever, Khun Daeng. Shove your Starbucks where the sun don't shine!" Daeng understood the sentiment, namely because he was already aware that most of the words Bob Lowe used were superfluous piffle.

The two older men chatted about their plans for the day. Daeng was feeling a bit lazy and said he would work for a few hours but then Toon would come and pick him up as she was taking him out to some fancy restaurant for dinner.

"Does she know you don't know anything about

fancy food?" Nat ribbed his old friend.

"I know how to eat. That's enough."

"Ahaan Thai! Marvellous!' Bob tried to get in on the act and chatting about ahaan Thai (Thai food) was a conversation he was very skilled and comfortable in. Fortunately for him, Thai people, Daeng and Nat included, never tired of chatting about food. It was one of the perks of living in the country with the world's greatest cuisine that one could always enthuse about it. Bob had lived in Thailand for over ten years but still felt he was learning about the culinary nuances and it was amazing how often he would still be introduced to new foods.

"Do you know, boys, my first five years in Thailand I never tried Yam Thua Plu." Yam Thua Plu, a Thai salad made with wing beans, eggs, and shrimps was now a Lowe favourite.

"It was life changing. Life changing. When I first tasted that salad it was without doubt one of the best days of my life. I almost get emotional thinking about it." Bob grinned and slurped his coffee noisily.

"Yes, delicious." Nat agreed.

"Unquestionably."

"Yes." Daeng spoke almost as a reflex.

These three sat in near silence, punctuated by the odd comment. Bob was now morphing into the group, making similar sounds and nods to the other two. The power of group dynamics. Bob was certainly easily influenced and suggestible and it would have been fascinating to a psychologist to study these three. Daeng himself had begun to adopt a few of Bob's phrases, and realising they had finished their coffees said, "More tea, vicar?"

Bob laughed heartily and noticed in the distance

Nont walking down the soi towards the three men. Game on, thought Bob. He had discussed the plans with Nont, or rather Pat had told Nont how to play it, and she was certain it would pan out as she expected.

Daeng recognised Nont. "Morning. How's your mother?"

"She's good. Same as ever, Khun Daeng. In fact that is why I am here. I need to ask you a favour."

"You're not stealing sweets from my shop I hope!" Nat chipped in, remembering when Nont was about six or seven he had caught him trying to distract Ning so he could take a one baht sweet. Nont laughed.

"My mother has no transport to take all her pork to the stall in the mornings." Nont dived straight in.

Daeng might have looked like a grizzled old uneducated man but he was wise enough to know where this was going, immediately.

"Oh. What's happened to the truck?"

Nont looked down. "I am waiting for some repairs, it may take a few weeks."

Daeng had a little glint in his eye when he asked, "So how can I help?"

Nont glanced towards the tuk-tuk. "I wonder if you would be prepared to do an early morning run every day. We'd pay you well of course."

Daeng shook his head. "I've seen what time your mother starts. Too early."

Nat nodded, way too early.

There was a short silence before Daeng looked up as if he had just had a masterful idea. "If you know how to drive my tuk-tuk, you could rent it from me, every morning, but I would need it back by seven at the latest."

Nont beamed. "Thank you so much. How much

would I need to pay you?"

"You pay whatever you can afford, young Nont." Daeng winked and Nont thanked him again before walking away.

"Remarkable," uttered Bob Lowe.

"Oh, you understood did you, Bob?" Daeng sarcastically enquired of his new friend.

"I think I picked up the gist, Daeng." Lowe smiled, and Daeng patted him hard on the back before shuffling inside to make a new pot of coffee.

Bob couldn't have felt happier. Pat was spot on. Everyone knew what was going on, but no one said anything. All was well.

"That fried pork his mother makes is delicious." Nat was thinking about crunching down on a crispy piece. "Delicious." Bob began to wander into the same daydream.

He texted Pat. *Tuk-tuk case reached an amicable conclusion. We did it, Pat. Lunch?*
Pat replied almost immediately. *We did it!*

They arranged to meet for lunch, Bob insisting that he had to have Yam Thua Plu, not open to negotiation. His final message, *No yam thua plu, no lunch.*

'The Bizarre Case of the Suicide Killer' – The next in the Bob Lowe Series, available now.

ABOUT THE AUTHOR

Zach J Brodsky spent much of his youth traipsing around the world where he was fascinated by observing people and creating absurd back stories in his mind about their lives. The result was the creation of an endless list of characters. He roamed around East and Southern Africa in the early 1990s sneaking into what was Zaire to spend some time with mountain gorillas, and later travelled extensively in South East Asia and the West Coast of the USA. Zach experimented with traditional employment for many years before deciding to base himself in Bangkok where he began to observe all the oddities that Bangkok has to offer, ultimately motivating him to try and patch some characters together in creating his first full novel "Bangkok Delusions".

Zach continues to roam the globe milling around South East Asia and quietly observing places and events that might inspire a new storyline.

For more information on Zach's books visit www.zachjbrodsky.com and sign up for advance notification on future releases.